THE WORKS OF LEONARD MERRICK

TO TELL
YOU THE TRUTH

The Works of

LEONARD MERRICK

TO TELL YOU THE TRUTH.

WHILE PARIS LAUGHED. Being Pranks and Passions of the Poet Tricotrin.

CONRAD IN QUEST OF HIS YOUTH. With an Introduction by SIR J. M. BARRIE.

WHEN LOVE FLIES OUT O' THE WINDOW. With an Introduction by SIR WILLIAM ROBERTSON NICOLL.

THE POSITION OF PEGGY HARPER. With an Introduction by SIR ARTHUR PINERO.

THE MAN WHO UNDERSTOOD WOMEN and other Stories. With an Introduction by W. J. LOCKE.

THE WORLDLINGS. With an Introduction by NEIL MUNRO.

THE ACTOR-MANAGER. With an Introduction by W. D. HOWELLS.

CYNTHIA. With an Introduction by MAURICE HEWLETT.

THE QUAINT COMPANIONS. With an Introduction by H. G. WELLS.

ONE MAN'S VIEW. With an Introduction by GRANVILLE BARKER.

THE MAN WHO WAS GOOD. With an Introduction by J. K. PROTHERO.

A CHAIR ON THE BOULEVARD. With an Introduction by A. NEIL LYONS.

THE HOUSE OF LYNCH. With an Introduction by G. K. CHESTERTON.

HODDER & STOUGHTON, Limited, LONDON.

TO TELL
YOU THE TRUTH
BY LEONARD MERRICK

 HODDER & STOUGHTON

LIMITED   LONDON

PRINTED IN GREAT BRITAIN BY
RICHARD CLAY & SONS, LIMITED,
BUNGAY, SUFFOLK.

CONTENTS

I

MADEMOISELLE MA MÈRE

SHE was born in Chauville-le-Vieux. Her mother gave piano lessons at the local Lycée de Jeunes Filles, and her father had been " professeur de violon " at the little Conservatoire. Music was her destiny. As a hollow-eyed, stunted child, who should have been romping in the unfrequented park, she had been doomed to hours of piano practice in the stuffy salon, where during eight months of the year a window was never opened for longer than it took to shake out the rug. Her name was Marie Lamande.

She had accepted her fate passively. If it had not been scales and exercises that made a prisoner of her, she recognised that it would have been fractions, or zoology. In France, schools actually educate, but few children have a childhood. On the first day of a term, when the wan girls reassemble, they sometimes ask one another—curious to hear what novelty the " holidays " may have yielded, amid the home work—" Did you have a little promenade during the *vacances*? "

Because its Lycée was widely known, English and American families came to stay in Chauville— the English pupils discovering what it was to be

B

taught with enthusiasm—and Marie knew French girls who had been initiated into the pleasures of tea-parties. Open-mouthed, she heard that the extravagant anglaise or américaine must have spent at least five or six francs on the cakes. But all the foreigners successively grew tired of inviting French children whose astonished mothers sent them trooping as often as they were asked, and, in no case, gave an invitation in return, and Marie herself never had the good luck to be asked.

Like her parents, she had been intended for the groove of tuition, and in due course tuition became her lot. But she was a gifted pianist, and ambitious; she dreamed of glory. Some years after she had been left alone, when her age was twenty-seven, she dared to escape from the melancholy town that she had grown to execrate. A slight little woman, without influence or knowledge of life, she aspired to conquer Paris. She attacked it with a sum sufficient to keep her for twelve months.

Her arrival at once frightened and enraptured her. In Chauville, at eight o'clock in the evening, a few of the shopkeepers had sat before their doorways, in the dark, a while; at nine, their crude streets were as vacant as the boulevards of the professional and independent classes, whose covert homes signified, even in the day-time, VISITORS WILL BE PROSECUTED. Behind the shutters of long avenues were over sixty thousand persons—most of them heroically hard-working—of a race that the pleasure-seeking English called " frivolous," content with no sem-

blance of entertainment but the ill-patronised performances provided by a gloomy theatre, which
was unbarred on only two days in the week.   Paris,
spirited and sparkling, in the tourist regions, took
her breath away.   Music called to her imperiously.
She sat, squeezed among crowds, at the recitals of
celebrities; and came out prayerful, to wonder:
" Will crowds ever applaud *me* ? "   But after the
first few days she reduced her expenses, and her
allowance for concert-going was strict.

She found a lodging now in the rue Honoré-
Chevalier, and sought engagements for Soirées d'Art
and Matinées Artistiques, writing to many people
who made no reply, and crossing the bridge to
appeal in person to many others, who were inaccessible, or rude.

Among the few letters of introduction that she
had brought from Chauville, one served its purpose.
Madame Herbelin, the Directrice of the Lycée,
always kindly disposed towards her, had recommended her to an acquaintance as a teacher.
Thanks to this, she earned five francs each Thursday
by a lesson.

When nine alarming weeks had slipped away
she gained an interview with a fat man who had
much knowledge, and who was interested in hearing
himself talk.   He said to her :

" Mademoiselle, it is a question of finances.   To
rise in the musical world you must give concerts,
and to give concerts you must have money.   Also,
you must have the goodwill of pupils in a position
to collect an audience for you, otherwise your

concerts will be a heavier loss still. Further, you must have the usual paragraphs and critiques : ' Triumph ! Triumph ! What genius is possessed by this divine artist, whose enchanting gifts revolutionise Paris ! Mademoiselle Lamande is, without question, the virtuosa the most *spirituelle*, the most *troublante* of our epoch.' These things do not cost a great deal in the Paris newspapers, but, naturally, they have to be paid for."

She told him : " I am a poor woman, and the only pupil that I have here is a child in Montparnasse."

The fat man, groaning comically, volunteered to " see what he could do."

He forgot her after five minutes.

Practising, in the feeble lamplight of the attic, she used to wait, through the long evenings, for the postman and news that never came. " For me ? " she would call over the banisters. " Nothing, mademoiselle ! " Then, back to the hired Pleyel, that barely left space for her to wash. Inexorable technique, cascades of brilliance, while her heart was breaking.

After she shut the piano, the dim light looked dimmer. The narrow street was silent. Only, in the distance sometimes, was the jog-trot of a cab-horse and the minor jangle of its bell.

Her siege of Paris made no progress.

Companionship came to her when ten months had gone. A young widow drifted to the house, and now and then, on the stairs, they met. One day they found themselves seated at the same table, in a little crémerie close by, and over their œufs-sur-le-plat they talked. As they walked home together, the widow said :

"I always leave my door open to hear you play."

The answer was, "Won't you come into my room instead?"

Madame Branthonne was a gentlewoman, employed in the Bernstein School of Languages. She was so free-handed with her sous, so generous in the matter of brioche and chocolate, that Marie thought she must be comparatively rich. But madame Branthonne was not rich; and when Marie knew her well it transpired that she remitted every month, out of her slender salary, for the maintenance of a baby son in Amiens.

"How you must miss him! How old is he?"

"Only eleven weeks. Miss him? Mon Dieu! But I had to leave him, or we should both have starved; if I had brought him with me, who would have looked after him all day while I was out? Besides, in this work, there is no telling how long one may remain in any city—I might be packed off to some other branch of the concern to-morrow."

"Really?"

"Oh yes; one never knows. Last week one of our professors was sent at a day's notice to Russia. What a life! Of course, one need not consent to go, but it is never prudent to refuse. You used to make me cry in there for my baby, when you played the piano. The poor little soul is called

' Paul,' after his father; he is with a person who
used to be my servant; she is married now, and
has a little business, a dairy. I know she is good
to him, but imagine how I suffer—in less than a
year I have lost my husband and my child. Alors,
vrai ! what an egotist I am ! How go your own
affairs ?   Still no luck ? ''

In the Garden of the Luxembourg on Sundays,
the two lonely women sauntered under the chestnut-
trees and talked of their sorrows and their hopes.
The hopes of the widow were centred upon the
lotteries *de Bienfaisance*, which had lured a louis
from her time and again.   She was emerging from
a period of enforced discretion, and she asked :
'' What do you say to our buying a ticket between
us ? ''

The present lottery had neared its end; only
one drawing remained, and the price of tickets was
accordingly much reduced.   The friends bought
their microscopic chance for five francs each.

The prizes that were dangled varied between
a mite and a fortune; and now, in the murky
lamplight of the garret, the pianist saw visions.
Rebuffed, intimidated, she had suddenly a prospect; chimerical as the prospect was, she might
gain the means to buy a hearing for her art !

For the woman seeking recognition, opportunity.
For the woman divided from her child, a home.
Every night they spoke of it.   Often while the
lamp burnt low, and a horse-bell jangled sadly,
they laughed together in a castle-in-the-air.

But those brats from the *Assistance publique*,

who blindly dispensed destinies at the drawing,
dipped their red hands upon the wrong numbers.

"As usual! I am sorry I proposed it to you.
It is an imbecility to waste one's earnings in such
a fashion—one might as well toss money in the
Seine. Well, I have had enough! I have finished.
I am determined never to gamble any more," cried
madame Branthonne, who had made the same
resolve a dozen times.

Marie said less. But her disappointment was
black; it was only now that she knew how vivid
had been her hope. And in the meanwhile her
little hoard had dwindled terribly, and she was
seeking other pupils.

"What if you get them—you will be no nearer
to renown? In Chauville you have a living waiting
for you—why wear out shoe-leather to find bread
in Paris? Poverty in Paris is no sweeter than
poverty elsewhere."

"If I go back to Chauville, it means the end,"
she answered. "I shall never have anything to
look forward to there—never, to the day of my
death. Year after year I shall sit teaching exercises and little pieces to schoolgirls who will never
play. The girls will escape, and marry, but *I* shall
sit teaching the same exercises and little pieces to
their children. Here, if I can hold out, if only I
can hold out long enough, I may batter my way
up. I want to get on—I've a right to get on.
You don't suppose that no one has ever made a
career who couldn't pay for it?"

"No," sighed her confidante; "I don't suppose

it's so bad as that—men do help one sometimes."
But in her heart she felt, " You aren't the kind of
woman that men do things for."

And, to a stranger, even pupils at five francs an
hour proved hard to find. A pianist of talent—
and she couldn't earn a living in Paris, even by
elementary lessons. It was one of those cases which
the uninitiated call " improbable," and which are
happening all the time.

Yet it fell to madame Branthonne to quit Paris
first. When Marie Lamande could no longer sleep
at night, or slept only to see the desolation of
Chauville in her dreams, the teacher of French was
required to go to one of the London branches of
the school. It occurred abruptly; the news and
the good-bye were almost simultaneous.

A new proclamation of millions to be won,
aggrandised " *par arrêté ministériel*," was blazoned
across the pages of the newspapers; and, on
impulse, the woman who was " determined never
to gamble any more " left a louis with the other,
to buy a ticket for her.

" You know you can't spare it," urged Marie.
" I wouldn't, if I were you ! "

Momentarily the widow hesitated; and then she
gave a shrug.

" Oh, of course, I'm an idiot," she exclaimed.
" But what else have I got to hope for ? Yes, get
it and send it to me ! "

Early in the journey she vacillated again. But
her instructions were not revoked, because soon
afterwards no more than a third of the train

remained on the rails, and madame Branthonne was among the victims killed.

Her aghast friend heard of the catastrophe twelve hours later than multitudes for whom it had no personal interest. Dazed, she wondered whether the ex-servant in Amiens would see the name of " Branthonne " in the list of the dead, and what would become of the baby now. She had a confused notion that she ought to communicate with the woman, but she was ignorant of the address. She went hysterically to the head office of the school, where the manager undertook to make inquiries at the Amiens branch.

When the sickness of horror passed, her thoughts reverted to the ticket that she had been enjoined to buy; and on the way to fulfil the duty, it was as if the dead woman, as she had seen her last, with her hat and coat on, were close to her again. " What name? " inquired the clerk in the big bank. " Lamande," she answered—and asked herself afterwards if it would have been more businesslike to say " Branthonne." But it didn't seem to matter. The point that perplexed her was, in whose charge ought the ticket to be? It belonged to the baby now, and its possibilities extended through the year. " Série No. 78, Billet No. 19,333." Ought she to post it confidingly to the dairy-keeper when she learnt where she lived?

The question persisted, as she tramped the streets despondently—as daily she drew nearer to defeat. She had discontinued to hire a piano. Everywhere she was humbled with the same reply, banished with the same gestures, maddened by the same callous unconcern. Paris was brutal ! She dropped in her purse the last louis that protracted hope. When this was gone, there would be left nothing but the price of her journey to Chauville and despair.

In the first drawing of the lottery, a few days later, the ticket won a prize of twelve thousand francs.

In a crumpled copy of *Le Petit Journal*, in the crémerie, she read of the drawing, by chance—not having remembered for what date it was announced. And she took a copy of the paper home with her— having forgotten the number of the ticket that she had bought. And when the revelation came to her, there was, blent with her thanksgiving for the child's sake, the human, bitter consciousness that, had she rashly suggested it, half the chance might have been hers. She might have stood here to-night on the threshold of success. So simple it would have been ! The knowledge was a taunt. She felt that Fate had robbed and derided her; she felt poor, as she had never felt poor before. . . .

The thought floated across her mind impersonally. It brought no shock, because it did not present itself as a temptation, even the faintest; it was just as if she had been recognising what somebody in a tale might do. Without purpose, without questioning why the thought fascinated her, she sat seeing how easily she could steal the money.

The ticket was on the table; there was nothing to show that she hadn't any right to it—she had

merely to claim the prize. There would be a fortnight's delay, at least, before she got it. Well,
she could eke out the sum that was put by for her
fare. She imagined her sensations on the morning
that she walked from the bank with notes for
twelve thousand francs in her pocket. If her pocket
were picked! Yielding even more intently to the
thought, she perceived that the proper course would
be to open an account before she left. . . . It
wouldn't be twelve thousand francs—a substantial
sum would be deducted for *les droits des pauvres*.
But it would be enough—the price of power! The
thought leapt further. She saw herself, gorgeously
gowned, on a platform—heard the very piece that
she was playing, the plaudits that came thundering;
she trembled in the emotion of a visionary fame.

Recalling her, there sounded, in the dark emptiness again, the minor jangle of a cab-horse bell.

Then she understood. It had been no idle
supposition, the thought that mastered her. " *O
divine Vierge Marie!* " she wailed on her knees,
and knew that she wanted to be a thief.

Through the night, through the morrow, through
every waking moment, a voice was saying to her:
" You *won't* be robbing a child; you can do for it
all that She did—every month, just the same thing.
Long before the child is old enough to need so
large a sum you will be in a position to give it to
him. What will he have lost? Nothing. You
are terrified by the semblance of a sin; it is not a
sin really. Dare it, dare it, be bold! "

Nothing could quell the voice. It was whispering

while she prayed. And the crashing of orchestras could not drown it, when she fled to music for relief.

She learnt that the woman in Amiens was called Gaillard, and had a shop in the rue Puteaux. But now she shrank from writing to her—she didn't know how she meant to act. Once, in desperation, she did begin a letter, an avowal of the prize that had been drawn; but she hesitated again.

There was an evening when, with steps that wavered, like a woman enfeebled by illness, she packed her things to return to Chauville. . . . She sat wide-eyed, staring at the trunk.

When she had dragged the things frantically out, she wrote to Amiens, making herself responsible for the monthly payments. " All that his mother did *I* will do ! " she wrote, feeling less criminal for the phrase. And then one morning, tortured, she caught the express to the town to see that all was well. The place was small and poor; and though the baby looked well cared for, and the young woman and her husband seemed kind, the visit was horrible to her. Next day she spent some of the stolen money on a baby's bonnet and pelisse. And as the quality of the gift suggested means, she received, before the date for her second remittance, a scrawl declaring that the cost of provisions had risen dreadfully, and asking for twenty francs a month more.

" Récital donné par Mademoiselle Marie Lamande." A blue-and-white poster, with her name staring Paris in the face. The time came

when she saw one on a wall, and stopped, thrilling
at it in the rain.   A week afterwards she saw one
on a wall again, and passed it with a sigh, remembering the half-empty salle, and the cheques that
she had drawn.

" Patience, mademoiselle, patience.   An artist
does not arrive in a day; one must persevere."
There were plenty of persons to give her encouragement now that it might be advantageous to
them.

But the expense of her début was a warning,
and she proceeded slowly.   Though they made her
feel very shy and cowardly, she did not succumb
to the arguments of vehement people who offered
" opportunities the most exceptional " at a big
price, and whose attitudes of amazement implied
that she must be brainless to decline.   She did not
waste money in bettering her abode.   She did not,
when she had given a recital again, continue to
imagine that the prize had provided a sum abundant
for her purpose.

The knowledge obsessed her that she owed this
money, that one day she was to repay it.   For a
year she told herself, " The road is harder than I
thought, but I shall reach the end of it in time ! "
During the second year she struggled in a panic,
while the money was melting, melting without
result.

To adventure a concert meant such wearisome,
such overwhelming preparation.   And within a
week it was as if it had never been—she was again
forgotten.   But she saw a little chorus-girl, who

had done something more than ordinarily immodest, launch herself into celebrity in a night.

At last, when she realised that she had wrecked her peace of mind for nothing, when to cross the bridge was to eye the river longingly, she knew that she wasn't free to find oblivion like that. Restitution to the child would be impossible, but it was her destiny to support him. She wrote to madame Herbelin, in Chauville, appealing for influence to regain the footing that she had kicked away. Her bent face was wet and ugly as she detailed the story of her failure; she foresaw the greetings, tactful, but galling, of acquaintances, the half-veiled satisfaction of other music-mistresses in the town.

The reply that reached her made it evident that to recover the position would be a slow process. And her means to wait were limited.

Hitherto the acknowledgments from Amiens had varied but slightly : " The remittance had come; the baby was well," or "the baby had had some infantile ailment, and was better." Now, a partially illegible letter informed her suddenly that the little business was to be given up. Circumstances compelled the woman to take a situation again, and she could not keep the orphan in her care. It was explained that " Mademoiselle should arrange to remove him in a month's time."

Already stricken, she was stupefied by this news. It seemed to her the last blow that could be dealt. What was to be done? She marvelled that she had not contemplated the contingency. She had

not contemplated it—at most, she had given it
a passing glance. She had questioned, agonised,
whether she could manage to maintain the payments regularly; she had asked herself what lay
before her when the child was older and his needs
increased; she had wondered, conscience-racked,
how she was to bear her life; but for this new
responsibility, hurled on her when she was broken,
she had been unprepared.

" Remove him? " To what? She wasn't remaining in Paris; was she blindly to answer some
advertisement before she left and leave a baby
behind her here, helpless in hands that might misuse
him? She shuddered. No; now that he would
be at the mercy of a stranger, the place must be
near enough for her to visit it—often and unex-
pectedly. She must find a place near Chauville.

But could she do it? However secretly she
arranged, wasn't it sure to be known? What was
she to say? It was a misfortune that she had
written to madame Herbelin too fully to be able to
assert now that she had married. What was she
to say? And who would credit what she said?

Hourly, the craven in her faltered that there
were hundreds of honest homes in Paris where he
would be gently treated, where he would be as safe
as he had been in Amiens. And always her better
self cried out : " But you'd desert him without
knowing that the home you had found was one of
them ! "

For three weeks she cowered at the crossways.

She did not love the little child that she had

wronged, as she bore him back with her to Chauville.
The journey was long, and he clung to her, whim-
pering, and she caressed him, white-faced and
abject; but there was no love for him in her heart.
The dusk, when they arrived, was welcome. She
led him down the station steps, her head sunk low.
In the street he cried to be carried, and she picked
him up—submissive to her burden. She had had
to sacrifice her reputation, or the child—and mademoiselle Lamande returned to her native town with
a baby in her arms.

She had booked to the Gare du Marché, the
station in the poorest quarter. A porter followed,
trundling the luggage over the cobbles. In a
narrow bed, under a skylight, the child and anxiety
allowed her little sleep.

Before she could begin her search for work, it
was imperative that she should find someone to
shelter him, if only during the day; and in the
morning she questioned a servant who was sweeping
the stairs. The girl looked as if she had been
picked from a dustbin, and clothed from a rag-bag,
but, compared with English girls of her class, she
had brilliant intelligence. She thought it probable
that the woman at the épicerie across the road
might be accommodating.

The woman at the épicerie was unable to arrange,
but she suggested a concierge of her acquaintance
" là bas." " Là bas " proved to be remote.
Chauville had not changed. As of old, the door of
the Église Ste. Clothilde was lost in its vast frame
of funeral black; as of old, the insistent bell was

dinning for the dead. The population was still concealed, except where a cortège of priests, and acolytes, and mourners wound their slow way with another coffin to the cemetery, Chauville's most animated spot.

As a makeshift, the concierge sufficed.

To gain an interview with madame Herbelin strained patience. But after the applicant had sat for a long while, with her feet on the sawdust of the salle d'attente, where an officer, and a marquise drooped resignedly, madame la Directrice told her : " It is a sad pity that you left the town." Marie could not remember that the busy woman said anything more valuable.

There was, however, another occasion. This time the lady said : " Mademoiselle, I knew you when you were a little girl, and I knew your parents, and I have regretted, more than you may suppose, that it was not in my power to offer you an appointment at the Lycée, in your emergency. But I have recently heard something about you that is very grave—something that I trust is not true."

" Madame," said Marie, trembling, " I can guess what you have heard, and it is *not* true. Only this is true—I have placed a child with a concierge in the rue Lecomte and go to see it there. It is the orphan of a woman who was my friend in Paris, a widow—we lived together."

Madame Herbelin did not speak.

" Madame Branthonne was killed in a railway accident, going to England," Marie went on; " she was a teacher in the Bernstein School. Her baby

C

had been left in Amiens, with a woman called
Gaillard. A few weeks ago the woman wrote to
me that she was going away, and was unable to
keep the child any longer. I couldn't abandon it
to the *Assistance publique*."

" Where is she now, this madame Gaillard ? "
inquired the Directrice coldly.

" I do not know," said Marie. And then, recognising the lameness of the reply, she burst forth
into a torrent of details to corroborate the story.

Her voice, more than the details, carried conviction to the listener. After a long pause she
said :

" Mademoiselle, I believe you have done a
generous thing." The thief winced. " But it was
an imprudent thing, a thing that you could not
afford to do. I do not speak of your intention to
maintain the child—may le bon Dieu aid you in
the endeavour ! But you did wrong to bring it
to Chauville. You should not expose yourself to
calumny. I counsel you most earnestly to place
the child somewhere else without delay."

" Madame, it is my duty to have him under my
own eyes," she urged. " Apart from me, he might
be starved, beaten, corrupted—my friend's boy
might be reared as an apache. How could I know ?
I should risk it all. It would be inhuman of me."

" I think you over-estimate the dangers," sighed
madame Herbelin. " In fine, if you put the boy
away from you, it is possible he may suffer. But
if you keep him near you, it is certain *you* will
suffer. I cannot say more."

" *I* must suffer," answered Marie.

A permanent home for him, not far from the rue
Lecomte, was found at a bonneterie, whose humble
little window contained Communion caps, and the
announcement " Piqures à la Machine."

To have had him in her lodging would have cost
her less.   But this child that dishonoured her must
be covert from the jeunes filles that she hoped
would come there; and if she had to give lessons
out, she could not leave him there alone.

She did have to give lessons out.   It was a
descent for her here to go to the pupils' houses,
but she was compelled to do it.   And something
bitterer—she was compelled to accept a lowered
fee, and affect to be unconscious why a reduction
was proposed.   To obtain the services of a " belle
musicienne " for a trifle, there were a few mothers
who engaged her, and replied to questioning relatives
that she was a " slandered woman."   But to her
they did not say that she was slandered, and their
hard eyes were an insult.

She gave a lesson twice a week for twenty francs
a month now, mademoiselle Marie Lamande, who
had advertised recitals in Paris, and she went short
of food, to meet the charges at the bonneterie.
The boy seemed to be amply nourished, and the
remembrance sustained her on the days when she
was dinnerless.

God! for a chance to get away, to be free of
this place, where it was an ordeal to tread the
streets.   When she could afford to buy a postage
stamp she applied for salaried work in some distant

school. Once it looked as if the child were not to
live; and as she sat, obeying orders, through one
endless night, she knew, before she fainted from
exhaustion, that if he died, her own escape from
Chauville would be made by the same road.

But he recovered—thanks partially to her—and
her duty still had to be done.

He recovered, and, as time passed, began to talk
like other children on the doorsteps. She recalled
the refinement of his mother, and the little child in
a black blouse, shrilling kitchen French, avenged
himself unknowingly. " As often as we ever meet,
when the boy I robbed is a poor, big, common
man," she thought, " every note of his voice will
be a chastisement ! "

Before she accomplished her release, she bore in
Chauville-le-Vieux a three-years' martyrdom.

Madame Herbelin had consented to testify to
her abilities, and she went far away, to a school
at Ivry-St.-Hilaire. She had pleaded that, in the
letter of recommendation, she might be referred to
as " madame " Lamande, but this entreaty the
Directrice would not grant.

" Mademoiselle," she said, " I cannot do it for
you; and if you are wise, there is no need.
Remember what I told you when you returned,
and be guided by me this time. Do not repeat
there the blunder that you made here. Leave the
child where he is; you have tested the person and
you know she is honest. Occasionally, once a year,
you can afford to come and see him. If you take
him with you, you will not gain much by your

removal. Of course, at Ivry-St.-Hilaire your
parentage is unknown and there is nothing to
hinder you from inventing a relationship; but it
isn't worth the trouble—believe me, you would be
suspected just the same. Make the most of this
opportunity; go unencumbered—do not live your
whole life in shadow for the sake of an ideal."

But her conscience would not allow her to see
him only once a year, nor to leave him to play on
the doorstep, and attend the École Communale.
In view of a constant salary, she already foresaw
herself alleviating his plight. She was resigned to
live her life in shadow, that she might yield a
little sunshine to him.

So, when she had sacrificed herself again, madame
la Directrice thought : " She is strangely devoted
to the child. I wonder if I was wrong to befriend
her—perhaps she is a bad woman, after all ! "

She did not venture to take the boy with her,
however. She was more than three months at
Ivry before her furtive arrangements for him were
concluded. Then she placed him with priests
twenty miles distant from her, in the Établissement
des Frères Eudoxie at Maison-Verte. Small as the
annual charges were, they were vast in relation to
her salary. Till she succeeded, by slow degrees, in
obtaining a few private pupils, her self-denial was
severe.

But the little chap was in better hands now.
And the woman had procured a respite from disdain.
A tinge of colour crept back into her cheeks, and
she faced the world less fearfully. By and by,

when she could afford the fare, she went to the
institution sometimes, on a Sunday, and walked
with him in the cour, and noted that gradually his
speech improved.   As she could afford the fare but
seldom, the intervals were long.

Paul looked forward to her rare visits.   Some of
the boys had visitors more frequently than he,
pale women who came to walk beside them in the
cour; and the boastful shout of " Ma mère ! " was
often humiliating to Paul.   He had been taught to
call her " mademoiselle," but one Sunday, the child,
in a triumphant cry, found his own name for her :
" *Mademoiselle ma mère est venue !* "

After that, he called her always " Mademoiselle
ma mère "; and, divining something of the little
wistful heart, mademoiselle did not reprove him.

At Ivry-St.-Hilaire a thing strange and bewildering happened.   For the first time in her life a man
sought her society; for the first time in her life
she was happier for talking to a man.   Two
moments were prodigious to her—a moment after
she had heard herself laughing merrily; a moment
when she realised why she had just plucked out a
grey hair.

When they were alone together one day the man
said to her :

" Now that I have made a practice in the town
at last, I am rooted here—and Ivry isn't amusing.
If a woman were to marry me she would have to
live here always.   I tell you this because I love
you."

It was as if God had wrought another miracle.

" I can't understand it," she whispered truly.

Then the man laughed and took her in his arms, and it seemed to her that she had never known what it was to be tired.

When he let her go and she came back to the world, her sin was staring at her. And now the voice that decoyed her before was clamouring: " If you degrade yourself in his sight you'll lose him."

Her lover appeared to her no less a hero because, under his imposing presence, he was a cur, and the thing that she feared would revolt him was her dishonesty.

Not on that day, nor on the next, but after many resolutions to do right had melted into terrors, she forced him to listen; and it seemed to her that she was dying while she spoke.

" I stole," she moaned, her face covered.

" Pauvrette ! " he exclaimed tenderly.

When she dared to look, he was smiling. The relief and gratitude in her soul were so infinite that she wanted to kneel at his feet.

But when she sobbed out the story of her later struggles and told him how she was devoting her life to the child, his brow grew dark.

" That, of course, would have to be changed," he said.

" Changed ? " she stammered.

" Obviously, best beloved. One must consider public opinion. These journeys to Maison-Verte are mad; they must cease. You have not been fair to yourself; and now, more than ever, you need to reflect that——"

"But," she broke in, frightened, "you don't understand. It is not a mere question of my going to Maison-Verte; he will not be there always—he will grow up, and his future will be my care. My responsibility goes on. Oh, I know—you need not tell me—that you have thoroughly the right to refuse, but—but I have no right to alter. Since I have seen that I could never hope to give back what I took, I have seen that he was my charge for life."

"Mon Dieu!" he said, "you exaggerate quixotic-ally. To give back what you took? Remember what you have already done!"

"Counted in francs," she pleaded, "I have done very little. It has been difficult to do, that's all."

Presently, when he perceived that, on this one point, the little weak woman was inflexible, the man made a beautiful speech, declaring that she was worth more than the opinion of Ivry-St.-Hilaire, and of all France. He said that nothing mattered to him but their "divine love." He looked more heroic still, and his eyes were moist with the nobility of the sentiments that he was delivering.

But as he sat in the principal café of the town by and by, among the stacks of swords in the corners, and the élite of the military and civil circles, clearing their throats vociferously on to the floor, he knew that a few days hence he meant to deliver a second lie about the "supplications of his family and his duty as a son." Had her debt been paid, he would have held her absolved from yielding so much as another thought to the boy, and he could have afforded to pay the debt, but it did not even enter his mind to commit such a madness. Yet, in his fashion, he loved her. The " chivalry " of offering marriage to a woman without a *dot* had proved it.

It would have been kinder to her not to leave her in a fool's paradise; she was to suffer more intensely because of that.

" Some of the facts, sufficient to explain the position, I have confided to my mother," he told her. " She is very old, and the honour of the family is very dear to her. I entreat you, in her name. The boy shall remain in this institution, or be placed in some other. They will teach him a trade. When the time comes for him to earn his living he will be no worse off than the other *gosses* there. Be guided by me. I assure you, you are morbidly sensitive. There is no reason why you should ever meet him again. My adored one, our happiness is in your hands. Give the child up ! "

" I cannot," she repeated hopelessly.

And then, all of a sudden, the imposing presence vanished and she saw the puny man—more clearly than he had ever seen himself.

" It begins to be plain why you ' cannot,' " he hissed. " Zut, tell your yarn about your ' theft ' to somebody greener. For *me* it's too thin ! . . . But why should we part, ducky? The matter could be arranged."

When he had demonstrated his intelligence in this way, without advantage, the man went down the garden path, out of her life—and for an hour she sat sightless, and ageing years. The birds in the garden were making a cruel noise. She felt that she had grown too old during the afternoon to bear the shrillness of the birds. When was it that she had had the arrogance to pull out a grey hair?

Her love-story was over; but the drear routine continued—the thrift, the drudgery, the clandestine journeys to the boy. If, when she saw him next, he felt that she was colder to him, she did not mean to be so. Never had she striven quite so wearily to be tender.

It was insensibly that she ceased to recall him as a burden. Had Time's touches been more swift she would have marvelled at the mystery of the thing. But the weight of life was lifted very slowly, and the burden bid fair to be consoling before she realised that the load was less.

As the months wore by, and term succeeded term, the boy evoked an interest in the loneliness. Duty no longer took her to him—it was affection; to amuse him now was not a task—their playtime had become her single pleasure. From this child, the woman who had had no childhood, captured gleams of youth—the virgin who was for ever celibate, caught glimpses of maternity. "In the *vacances*, Paul, I'll come and stay at Maison-Verte," she used to say, "and we'll have picnics in the park!" When the *trimestre* was over and she studied his report, her smile was proud. Once when she went, he rushed to meet her with a prize. " Mademoiselle ma mère, look, look ! " he halloed. And the virgin's arms were flung about him and she hugged him like a mother.

As a mother she marked his progress, year by year; as a mother, mourning his barren prospects and craving to advance them, she beat her breast that she had made him penniless. It was as a mother that, by parsimonies, protracted and implacable, she garnered the means at last to better his condition. By this time her hair was all grey, and the schoolboy's voice was breaking.

On the day that she was strong enough, she meant to confess to him and see his love turn to contempt. But the day when she was strong enough wouldn't come. When he was sixteen she had said : " I shall tell him in a year from now ! " When he was seventeen she had wept : " God couldn't mind his loving me for a year more ! "

" Mademoiselle," he would say—for he was a young man and had dropped the other name—" I don't know why you have been so good to me." And she would answer : " Your mother and I were friends, dearest." Only that.

" You work too hard," he would declare, " ever so much too hard; you're always tired. You know, you weren't ambitious enough—that was your great mistake. You shouldn't have gone in for teaching; you ought to have played at concerts—you might have been no end of a swell. Play something to me now, will you? What used my mother to say about your playing ? "

" She said once that it made her cry for her

baby, Paul. What do *you* think of when I play ? ''

But he was shy of admitting what he thought of, because he thought of noble deeds, and his ideal woman, and of the ecstasy it would be to see his name on the cover of a book—and he was doomed to be a clerk.

Yet when the clerk chafed in his bonds, and the conceit of authorship was too mighty to be bridled, it was to her that he first revealed a manuscript. It was she, trembling, who was his first critic. " Your good women are all perfect," she told him, " and your bad women have never a good impulse. We aren't like that." But she was never too weary to talk about the tales; and when they began to wander among august journals that refused them, she used to pray, before the crucifix in her bedroom, that the hearts of editors might be moved.

Now she meant to confess to him before he entered on his military service.

The parting was so bitter that she failed at the last moment. He went far from her. The years of his service were a much greater hardship to her than to him. During the first week she stinted her own diet to send a *bon de poste* to ameliorate his food; but he wouldn't keep the money. In the avenues of Ivry, never did she see the pitifully garbed conscripts being drilled without picturing the conscript who was dear to her, garbed like that—and closing her eyes with the pain.

And when he was free to return, the meeting was so sweet that she was a coward once more.

He was a clerk for a long time, but his dis-satisfaction would have been longer still without her. She it was who took to the *Echo d'Ivry-St.-Hilaire* the article that paved his way to journalism. There was a day of sovereignty when he was offered an ill-paid post on that undistinguished paper. How victoriously he twirled his moustache ! How proudly, through her spectacles, she watched him do it !

Oh, of course he wouldn't be content to stick for ever on the Ivry *Echo*, not he ! He was going to write great novels just the same. Incipiently the women of his stories lived now, but he was still very young. She said to him at this stage : " You put your girls in a drawing-room, but they come from a tavern." And, abashed and wondering, he saw that poor mademoiselle knew more of girl-hood than a literary man had learnt. He was an artist, or he would not have seen.

Because he was an artist he probed his questions deep. Because she loved him she did not flinch. To him she voiced truths that she had shrunk from owning to herself. Thoughts that had frightened her, and thoughts that she had deemed too sacred to be uttered, she brought forth for his guidance. Her innocence and her knowledge she yielded to him, her vanities and her regrets. She bared the holiest secrets of her sterile life and stripped her soul, that he might make his books of it.

But always there remained the one secret that she could not tell.

After he had begun to get on—when he was a

journalist in Paris—she had a terrible grief. She had travelled to Paris to see him, and he declined to admit her. He declined to admit her because he knew what she had come to say, and, under Heaven, there was nothing to him so precious as an idol that he had made out of a spiritual profile and some vices. The Ivry editor had told her it was rumoured that the woman talked of marrying Paul, and mademoiselle had written imploring letters to him without avail. " He must be the best judge of his own mind," he had answered, " and of the true nature of the woman he loved."

Then, distraught, she had made the journey, and been turned from the door with a servant's transparent lie. The tumult of the modern traffic confused her—the failing little figure was jostled by the crowd. She went, deafened, through remembered gates, to a bench, and sat there, feeling stunned. The bench was in the Garden of the Luxembourg, where it seemed to her that in another life she had walked beside his mother.

She had to save him. When her mind cleared, she thought only of that. Since it was impossible to plead to Paul, she must plead to the woman. She would find out where she lived ; she would say—— In imagining herself in the presence of such a woman, she was as timorous as a child. She would say—what ? The wildness of the notion overwhelmed her. Suddenly she felt that she could say nothing, that she would be tongue-tied, a sight for ridicule.

But she must save Paul !

She was two days in Paris before she obtained
the address; and she was no less amazing to the
wanton than was the wanton to the spinster. From
different worlds they marvelled at each other across
a hearthrug. She said :

" He is not my son, but he is as dear to me as if
he were; indeed, the sons of many women are far
less to them, I think, than he to me. I worked
for him when he was a baby. Since he has been a
man, he has meant the only interest in my life; it
has been a wretched failure of a life—the one hope
left in it is to see him succeed. Madame, his
career is in your hands. I entreat you to be
merciful—I beg it of you on my knees. I don't
pretend to judge your feelings for him, but if you
care for him really and deeply, do what you know
is right for the man you love—make a memory for
yourself that you'll be proud of. You're beautiful
now, and young, and you don't take some things
very earnestly, but one day, when you're older and
memories are all you've got, a noble remembrance
will be sweet. You'll say to yourself : ' *I* saved a
man from ruining his future, *I* saved a woman
from breaking her heart.' "

After her curiosity in the alien was exhausted,
the beauty rang the bell, and said :

" What kind of a fool are you to have imagined
I should give up a man I liked, because a stranger
asked me to? It's about the silliest idea I ever
heard of."

And then she herself did something sillier. She
told Paul what had happened, mimicking the

suppliant's sorrow, and jeering at her prayer. The man read into the scene the pathos that the jeerer missed, and he saw that the woman he had idealised lacked the grace of pity.

Later, when success came to him, there was no domestic tragedy darkening the home behind it, and he had owed to mademoiselle a timely rent in the veil of his illusion.

She was teaching at Ivry still when his success came. For weeks she had known by his letters, and the papers, that his new book had made a reputation for him, but one morning she heard that it was " making him rich." The hard times were over for them both, he wrote. There was to be no more labour for her, no more loneliness; they were to live together in a little appartement in Passy. She was to rest, " with flowers in the window, and her hands in her lap—he was coming to carry her away."

The letter quivered as she read it, and she put it down, in fright. The secret that had smouldered while she toiled for him, while she worked to keep herself, flared menace now that he proposed to keep her. She dared not accept her comfort of his ignorance. She saw herself as a cheat who had hidden her sin, a hypocrite who had taken gratitude to which she had no claim. Now he must be told. The confession that had terrorised her all her life could be escaped no longer; the day of her Calvary was here.

At every step in the street she shuddered, though it was not till evening that he was due. She clasped him, crying with pride and fear, when he strode in. He rattled gaily of things triumphant, things too difficult to-day for her to understand. She thanked God that it was twilight and he couldn't clearly see her face. She crept away from him and bowed her head. The young man looked forward. The old woman looked back.

In the twilight her confession came at last—in the twilight, his reverent knowledge of his boundless debt.

"But I have loved you," she sobbed. "At the beginning you were my punishment, but then I loved you!"

"You have borne want for me, and contempt. I have taken your youth from you, and your happiness and your strength." He went to her, and knelt, and kissed the trembling hands. "How *I* love *you*," he cried, "mademoiselle ma mère!"

D

II

ARIBAUD'S TWO WIVES

IN the Bois, one day, I met madame Aribaud.
By madame " Aribaud " I mean the wife of a very
popular dramatist, and I call them Aribaud
because it wouldn't do to mention their real name.
I like meeting madame Aribaud when I am in
Paris. It refreshes me, not only because she isn't
preceded by a gust of scent, and doesn't daub her
mouth clown red, like so many Parisiennes, but
because she is so cheerful. She diffuses cheerful-
ness. She sat beaming at her little son, while he
scattered crumbs for the birds, and she informed
me—it was in 1912—that he was in the latest
fashion, having a nurse from England to give him
the real English pronunciation, though as yet he
was hardly a linguist. And the nurse said, " I
tell madam we must be pietient with 'im; we can't
expect 'im to talk like I do hall at once."

Also the lady informed me that they had finished
arranging their new house, and that on the morrow
I must go there to déjeuner. Very readily I
went, and they showed me the " English nursery,"
and an American contrivance that she had presented to her husband for his dressing-room—
" *Comme ils sont pratiques, les américains !* "—and

an antique or two that she had picked up for his study; and, not least, she showed us both some croquettes de pommes that looked ethereal and— I have never tasted croquettes de pommes like madame Aribaud's! I always say she is the most domesticated of pretty women, and her husband the most pampered of good fellows. Playgoers who know him merely by his comedies, in which married people get on together so badly up to the fourth act, might be surprised to see inside his villa.

Only when he and I were lounging in the study afterwards—my hostess was in the little garden, pretending to be a horse—I said to him, as the boy's shouts came up to us through the open window, "Doesn't the child disturb you out there when you're busy?"

My friend nodded. "Sometimes," he acknowledged, "he disturbs me. What would you have? He must play, and the ' garden ' is too diminutive for him to go far away in it. It makes me think of what Dumas père said when he paid a visit to his son's châlet in the suburbs—' Open your dining-room window and give your garden some air!' Once or twice I have wondered whether I should work in a front room, instead, but to tell you the truth, I always come to the conclusion that I like the noise. Believe me, a dramatist may suffer from worse drawbacks than a child's laughter." He blew smoke thoughtfully, and added, " I had a wife who was childless."

Now, though I knew Maurice Aribaud very well

indeed, I had never heard that this was his second
marriage, and I suppose I stared.

" Yes," he said again, " I had a wife who was
childless." And then, with many pauses, he told
me a lot that I had not suspected about his life,
and though I can't pretend to remember his precise
words, or the exact order in which details were
forthcoming, I am going to quote him as well as
I can.

" I had not two louis to knock together when I
met her—and I wasn't so very young. I had been
writing for the theatre for years, and had begun
to despair of ever seeing anything produced. To
complete my misery, I had no companionship, if
one excepts books—no friend who wrote, or
aspired to write, no acquaintance who did not
draw his screw from a billet as humdrum as my
own. I was a clerk in the Magasins du Louvre, and
though of course the other men in the office talked
about plays—in France everybody is interested in
plays; in England, I hear, you are interested only
in the players—none of them was so congenial that
I was tempted to announce my ambitions to him.
I used to think how exciting it must be to know
authors and artists, even though they were obscure
and out-at-elbows. Every night, as I walked home
and passed the windows of a bohemian café I used
to look at it wistfully. I envied the fiercest
disappointments of the habitués inside, for they
were at least professionals of sorts; they moved on
a different planet from myself. Once in a blue

moon I found the resolution to enter, pushing the
door open timidly, like a provincial venturing into
Paillard's. I suppose I had a vague hope that
something might happen, something that would
yield confidences, perhaps a comrade for life. But
I sat in the place embarrassed, with the air of an
intruder, and came out feeling even lonelier than
when I went in.

" One windy, wet day I was at the mont-de-
piété to redeem my watch. I had pawned it two
or three weeks before, because I had seen a second-
hand copy of a book that I wanted very much and
couldn't afford at the moment. I will not inquire
whether you have ever pawned anything in Paris,
yourself, but if you haven't, you may not know the
formalities of the *dégagement*. Ah, you have
pawned things only in London.

" Well, after you have paid the principal and the
interest, you are given a numbered ticket, and then
you go into a large room and take your choice
among uncomfortable benches, and wait your
turn. It is something like cashing a cheque at
the head office of the Crédit Lyonnais, only at the
mont-de-piété the people on the benches sit waiting
for the most disparate articles. On one side of
you, there may be a fashionably dressed woman who
rises to receive a jewel-case—and on the other,
some piteous creature who clutches at a bundle.
The goods and chattels descend in consignments,
and when one consignment has been distributed,
the interval before the next comes down threatens
to be endless. The officials behind the counter

converse in undertones, and you meanwhile have nothing livelier to do than listen to the rain and wonder how hard-up your neighbour may be.

" That day, however, I did not chafe at the delay. There was a young girl there whose face caught and held my attention almost immediately. Not only was her prettiness remarkable—her expression was astonishing. She looked happy. Yes, in the gaunt room, among the damp, dismal crowd, relieving the tedium by a heavy sigh or an occasional shuffling of their shoes, this fair-haired, neat, innocent little girl looked happy. Smiles hovered about her lips, and her eyes sparkled with contentment. I tried to conjecture the reason for her delight, what treasured possession she was about to regain. A trinket? No, something indefinable in her bearing forbade me to think it was a trinket. My imagination ranged over a dozen possible pledges, without finding one to harmonise with her. Ridiculous as it sounds, I could picture nothing so appropriate for her to recover as a canary, which should fly, singing, to her finger. Every time a number was called, curiosity made me hope that her turn had come. The latest load that had been delivered was almost exhausted. Only three packages remained. Another call, and she got up at last ! The package was a bulky one. I craned my neck. It was a typewriter.

" Quite five minutes more lagged by before I got my watch, and when I crossed the courtyard I had no expectation of seeing her again; but no

sooner had I passed through the gate than I discovered her in trouble. She had been trying to
carry the typewriter and an open umbrella, and now
the umbrella had blown inside out, and she had
put the typewriter on the pavement.

"In such a situation it was not difficult for me to
speak.

"I picked the thing up for her. She thanked
me, and made another ineffectual attempt to depart.
I offered my help. She demurred. I insisted.
We made for her tram together—and tram after
tram was full. It had been raining for several
hours and Paris was a lake of mud. In the end I
trudged beside her through the swimming streets,
carrying her typewriter all the way to the step of
her lodging. So began my courtship.

"She was as solitary as I; her father's death had
left her quite alone. He had been old, and very
poor. Blind, too. But his work had been done up
to the last, my little sweetheart guiding him to the
houses—he had earned a living as a piano-tuner.
In Sèvres she had an aunt, his sister-in-law; but
though the woman boasted a respectable business
and was fairly well-to-do, she had come foward
with nothing more substantial than advice, and the
orphan had had only her typewriter to keep the
wolf from the door. Her struggles in Paris with a
typewriter! She had been forced to pawn it
every time she lost a situation. But every time
she saved enough to recapture it she felt prosperous again. Her own machine meant 'luxuries.'
With her own machine she could afford a plant to

put in her attic window, and a rosebud for her breast.

" She loved flowers, and she often wore them, tucked in her bodice, after the Magasins du Louvre closed—the lonely clerk used to hurry to meet the little typist on her way home. Yet she told me once that her love for them had come very late; for years the sight of all flowers had saddened her. She had been born on that melancholy boulevard that leads to the cemetery of Père La Chaise, that quarter of it where one sees, exposed for sale, nothing but floral tokens for the mourners—nothing to right and left but mountains of artificial wreaths, and drear chrysanthemums in stiff white paper cones. As a child she had thought that flowers were grown only for graves.

" I recall the courtship in all seasons, and always in the streets—when the trees were brown and the light faded while we walked; and when the trees had whitened and the lamps were gleaming; and when the trees grew green and we walked in sunshine. It was in the streets that we fell in love—in the streets that I asked her if she would marry me.

" We were on the quai des Orfèvres one Sunday afternoon in summer. I had meant to wait till we were in the Garden of the Tuileries, but we had stopped to look at the river, and—— I can see it all now, the barge folk's washing hanging out to bleach, and a woman knitting among the geraniums on a deck. There was a little fishing-tackle shop, I remember, called ' Au Bon Pêcheur,' and a poodle and a Persian cat were basking together on the doorstep. Our hands just touched, because of the people passing; and then we went on to the Tuileries, and talked. And before we seemed to have talked much, it was moonlight; a concert had begun, and away in the distance a violinist was playing *La Précieuse*. ' Why,' I exclaimed, ' I've given you no dinner ! ' She laughed; she hadn't been hungry, either. No millionaires have ever dined at Armenonville more merrily than we, for a hundred sous, at a little table on a sidewalk.

" She said, ' When I am your wife, I shall type-write all your plays for you, Maurice—perhaps that will bring you luck.' And by and by, when we came to the Magasins du Louvre, she pointed to the Comédie-Française : ' You haven't far to travel to reach it, dearest ! ' she smiled—' we'll cross the road together.'

" How sweet she looked in the wedding frock that she had stitched ! How proud I was of her ! Our ménage was two rooms on the left bank; and in the evening, in our tiny salon on the sixth floor, her devoted hands clattered away on her machine, transcribing my manuscript, till I kissed and held them prisoners. Didn't she work hard enough all day for strangers, poor child ?—my salary was too small to liberate her. ' You are jealous,' she would say gaily, ' because I write your dialogue so much faster than you.' And often I wished that I could create a scene as rapidly as she typewrote it. But we had our unpractical evenings, also, when we built castles-in-the-air, and chose the furniture for them. I had brought home, from the Magasins,

one of the diaries that they issue annually. It
contained plans of the theatres—it always does—
and, perched on my knee, she pictured a play of
mine at each of them in turn, and the house rocking
with applause. And then we pencilled the private
box we'd have; and drove, in fancy and our auto-
mobile, to sit there grandly on the three-hundredth
night.

" We spent many hours in selecting presents that
I would have made to her if I could. One of the
things she wanted was, of course, a theatre bag :
' the prettiest that you can pretend ! ' and I
pretended a beauty for her in rose brocade—and
inside I put the daintiest enamelled opera-glasses
that the rue de la Paix could show, and a fan of
Brussels point, and a Brussels-point handkerchief,
and a quaint gold bonbonnière with sugared violets
in it. I remember she threw her arms round my
neck as ecstatically as if the things were really
there. We were, at the time, supping on stale
bread, with a stick of chocolate apiece."

The dramatist sat silent, his eyes grown wide.
I think that for a moment he had forgotten his new,
desirable home and the antiques on the mantelpiece—that he was back in a girl's arms in a room
on a sixth floor. Under the window, his wife had
ceased to play at horses, and was swinging their son,
instead. The child's delight was boisterous.

She called up to us now : " Are we a nuisance,
messieurs ? Shall we go to the nursery ? "

" No, no," cried Aribaud, starting, " not at all;

we are doing nothing. Continue, mon ange, continue ! ''

" What a heaven opened," he went on, turning to me, " when I had a piece taken at last ! As long as I live I shall think of the morning that letter came, of our reading it together, half dressed, and crying with joy. She was making the coffee for breakfast. And yet, even when the contract was signed, it sometimes seemed incredible. I used to dream that it had happened, and dream that I was dreaming—that I was to wake and find it wasn't true. And the eternity of delay, the postpone-ments, one after another ! And then, when we felt worn out with waiting, the night that we jolted to the show in an omnibus, and sat breathless in the fauteuils de balcon ! I remember the first laugh of approval that the audience gave, her clutching my hand; and how she clung to me, sobbing and comforting, when we got home and knew that the piece had failed.

" I had a short run the next autumn with *Successeur de Son Père*, but my first hit, of course, was *Les Huit Jours de Léonie*. When that was produced, the fees came tumbling in.

" Weren't we dazed at the beginning ! And how important we felt to be taking a flat and going to a bureau de placement to engage a servant ! We were like children playing with a doll's-house. The change was marvellous. And when I received an invitation from somebody or other who had been unapproachable only a year before—her exultance to see me go! The invitations to the author, you understand, did not always include his wife; and, unfortunately, those that ignored her were often those that it would have been unwise for me to decline. I found that rather pathetic; we had hoped together for so long, and now that success had come she wasn't getting her fair half of the fun. An elaborate evening gown that we had hurried expectantly to order for her was not needed, after all—it was out of fashion before she wore it. Still, as I say, she exulted to see me go—at first. And later—— Well, when I insisted on a refusal because she had not been asked, it grieved her that I neglected opportunities for her sake; and when I consented to go without her she was, not unnaturally, dull.

" It was not very lively for her in the daytime, either. When my duties as a clerk had taken me from her, she, too, had had employment, but now, of course, her berth had been resigned, and while I wrote all day upstairs, she was alone. She was not used to leisure—all her life she had worked. We had no child to claim her time, to occupy her thoughts and yield the interests of maternity. Though she endeavoured to create distractions for herself, the flat that we had been so proud of was rather dreary for her, after its novelty faded. She sighed in it oftener than she laughed.

"The very few women that she met were actresses, who talked of nothing but their careers—their genius, their wrongs, and their Press notices. What companion could she find among them, even

had I wished her to seek their companionship?
And the men who came to us also talked shop
continuously, and directed themselves chiefly to
me. No doubt they would have had enough, and
too much, to say to her had I been absent, but, as
it was, they often appeared to forget that she was
there. As time went on, too, the theatre made
more and more demands upon me—a comedy in
rehearsal while another was being written; the
telephone bell always ringing to call me away just
when I had arranged to take a half-holiday with
her. And when I left the theatre I could not
dismiss the anxieties of a production from my mind
as I had dismissed the affairs of the Magasins
when I left my office stool—they were mine,
and I brought them home with me. She grew
bored, restless. She was nervy with solitude, and
chagrined at feeling herself insignificant. She told
me one day that she wanted me to put her on the
stage.

"Mon Dieu! To begin with, she had no gift
for the stage—and if she had been ever so clever,
did I want to see her there? I was aghast.

"'But, mignonne,' I said, 'what makes you
think, all of a sudden, you could act? Leaving
everything else aside, what reason is there to suppose you would succeed? You have had no
experience, you have never even shown the slightest
tendency towards it.'

"'I want something to do,' she said.

"'But,' I said, 'that isn't enough. And besides,
you would not like it at all—you would find it

" ' The days are longer than they used to be; I want something to do,' she insisted.

" Oh, I understood ! But I need hardly tell you that this fever of hers didn't make for bliss. The theatre became a bone of contention between us—the position that I had dreamed of and yearned for was dividing me from my wife. It got worse every year. I no longer dared to mention business in my home. We were on affectionate terms only in the hours when the theatre was forgotten. One day I would hold her in my arms, and on the next some chance allusion would estrange us. If I happened to come across a little actress who was suitable to a more conspicuous part than those that she had had hitherto, my casting her for it was a domestic tragedy—I ' made opportunities for every woman but one ! ' I have been told that strangers who pestered me for theatrical engage-ments complained that I was unsympathetic—they little guessed how I was pestered for engagements on my own hearth !

" The aunt at Sèvres also had something to say. She had managed to get on a semi-friendly footing with us when *Les Huit Jours* was running, and now she had the effrontery to take the tone of a mother-in-law with me. She ' knew I was devoted to her niece, but I was not being fair to her—I ought to realise that she had a right to a career, too.' What audacity !—a woman who had given nothing but phrases when her niece was penniless ! I did not wrap up my answer in silver paper—and I fancy the aunt's influence was responsible for a good deal; I think she revenged herself by offering all the encouragement possible behind my back.

" Anyhow, my wife announced to me at last that she had determined to go her own road without my help. It was as if she had struck me.

" She meant to seek an opening in some minor company in the provinces—in the obscurest of the théâtres ambulants, if she could do no better. It sounded so mad that at first I could hardly believe she was in earnest. The doggedness of her air soon convinced me; I would have welcomed the wildest hysteria in preference. Since I refused to further her ambition, she must resign herself to beginning in the humblest way, she told me quietly; she ' regretted to defy my wishes, but she was a woman, and I had been wrong to expect from her the blind obedience of a child—she could not consent to remain a nonentity any longer ! ' She dumfounded me. It meant actual separation, it meant the end of our life together—and she was telling me this composedly, coolly, as if our life together were the merest trifle, compared with the fascination of the footlights. I cursed the footlights and the day I first wrote for them. I swear I wished myself back in the Magasins du Louvre. My excitement was so violent that I could not articulate; I stuttered and stood mute. I went from her overwhelmed, asking myself what I was to do.

" There is one course that never fails to remedy marital unhappiness and bring husband and wife together again—on the stage. It is when he leads

E

were with her predecessor; I was mourning the love-
story that had begun like an idyll, and that seemed
to have had so bad an end.

The man's voice brought me back. " Yes, the
infallible situation had failed," he repeated. " What
do you suppose was the sequel? "

" I suppose," I sighed, " she had her way? "

" No," said Aribaud; " she had her baby."
He waved a triumphant hand towards the garden.
" And from the first promise of that God-sent gift,
the glamour of the theatre faded from her mind and
she talked only of her home. From that day to
this we have been as happy together as you see
us now."

My exclamation was cut short by the hostess
whose history I had been hearing.

" Messieurs, are you really sure we aren't laughing
too much for you? " she pealed up to us again.

" Sure, sure! It is well—it is as it should be—
we come to join you," shouted Aribaud. " Laugh
loud, my love—laugh on! "

III

THAT VILLAIN HER FATHER

HENRI VAUQUELIN was a widower with one daughter, to whom he had denied nothing from the time she used to whimper for his watch and drop it on the floor. So, after she left the convent where she had been educated, and told him how much she was missing her friend Georgette, he said gaily, " Mais, ma petite, invite mademoiselle— whatever her name may be, to come to Paris and stay with us for a month."

His gaiety was a trifle forced, however. Though he was happy to give his daughter a companion, he was pained to learn that his own companionship hadn't been enough. " For I have done all I could," he mused. " The fact is, that though I feel fairly young, I am elderly. That's the trouble. To a girl of twenty-one, a father of forty-five is an ancient for the chimney corner. I must see about finding her a husband—I shall have to talk to madame Daudenarde about her son the first time I am in the neighbourhood." And after Blanche had flung her arms round his neck, and darted forth to send the invitation to her friend, he surveyed his reflection in a glass pensively, and noted that his moustache was much greyer than he had thought.

When the indispensable Georgette arrived, in a costume that became her admirably, and sat at dinner, in a dress that became her more admirably still, replying to him with composure and point, he was surprised at the girls' attraction for each other—and his surprise did not diminish as the days passed. Though not actually more than two or three years older than Blanche, mademoiselle Paumelle was in tone much older. Blanche was an ingénue; Georgette was a woman. Excepting in moments, when she romped like a schoolgirl, all spontaneity and high spirits.

" She is a queer compound, your chum," he remarked when she had been with them for a fortnight. " Alternately thirty, and thirteen ! "

" You don't like her, papa ? "

" Oh, yes, she is well enough, and not bad-looking. I am relieved she did not turn out to be ugly—that would have depressed me. But it is a trifle confusing to be uncertain whether I am about to be addressed by a woman of the world or a madcap from a nursery."

" She used always to be a madcap till she lost her mother—you see, there are only her stepfather and his two sisters now. It is that that has changed her so dreadfully."

" I find nothing ' dreadful ' about her," said Vauquelin a shade sharply. " On the contrary, it—I suppose some people might find it rather fascinating. I merely observe that she is different from any other girl that I have met. What's the matter with her stepfather ? "

" She tells me he never stops talking."

" His topics must be pretty catholic. This
jeune fille from the country appears to know more
of politics, finance, society, and sport than I, who
have lived in Paris forty-five years."

" How you do exaggerate, papa!" rippled
Blanche reprovingly.

" At any rate, I do not exaggerate the years,"
sighed Vauquelin. " Well, if she is not happy at
home, why not ask her to stay with us for *two*
months? She is not in my way, you know."

But mademoiselle Paumelle declared that it
would be impossible for her to prolong her visit.
Blanche reported this to him with wistful lips, and
he said, " I'll see if *I* can persuade her—I will speak
to her about it in the morning when you go to take
your music-lesson."

On the morrow, " Blanche tells me that she is
greatly disappointed," he began. " She will miss
you terribly when you leave us, mademoiselle. I
wish you would think over your objection."

" It is infinitely kind of you, monsieur Vauquelin.
I fear that a month is the very most I can manage."

" Even to do us a service?"

" Ah, a ' service '!" She smiled. " You will
find plenty of people ready to do you such services."

" Not plenty of mesdemoiselles Paumelle. I am
in earnest. It is dull here for Blanche, alone with
me. I have done my best for her, I am not
consciously selfish—I have sat at home when I
wanted to go out, and gone out when I wanted to
stop at home. I have taken her to the Français

and pretended to enjoy myself, though I could have yawned my head off, and the question of her clothes has absorbed me more than the affairs of France. But I am old. All my tenderness for her cannot alter that."

" You do not seem to me old," said mademoiselle Paumelle.

" Don't I? " said Vauquelin, regarding her gratefully. " Look how grey my moustache is getting. And yet, do you know, when we're all laughing together I feel as young as ever I was."

" Your manner *is* young. The face alters ever so long before the manner."

" I am forty-f—er—over forty, and Blanche is twenty-one. What will you? I must get her married soon. It is my paramount desire. I rather fancy that Daudenarde and she may not dislike each other—the gentleman you saw the other evening."

" She was doing her hair from seven o'clock till eight, and he sighed when he handed her the lemonade."

" Your observation is invaluable. I must have a chat with his mother soon. It would be an excellent match. In the meantime she stands in need of the companionship and counsel of a young lady like you; she needs it most urgently. If your stepfather can spare you——"

" Ah, my stepfather could spare me for ever," she put in; " there are others to listen to him."

" And if you are not bored here——"

" Bored? I am having the time of my life."

" Eh bien? Remain for two months, I beg. Be merciful to us. I need your advice, myself. There is a matter that is harassing me : I cannot determine whether her new jumper should be beaded, silk-broidered, or fringed."

" If it is telling on your health——" Her eyes laughed into his.

" You yield? "

" I weakly wobble."

" There is, further, the consuming question of a simple evening dress—what it should be made of."

" I succumb. Tulle would be all right, or georgette."

" It shall be georgette—we shall not lose you so utterly when you go."

" Oh, you *are*—priceless ! " she pealed.

Vauquelin reflected, " She has three sterling qualities, this girl—she is pretty, she is nice, and she looks at me as if I were a young man."

During the next six weeks Vauquelin developed a zest for the Français that was astonishing. And not for the Français only, or for the Opéra Comique, and concerts, and kinemas. Blanche had never applauded her papa so ardently. He would be seized with captivating whims for expeditions, and picnics, and moonlight runs in the car. His frolicsomeness passed belief.

Not till the six weeks were over and mademoiselle Paumelle had departed, bearing Blanche with her, did his spirits fall. And then there would have been no buyers. The middle-aged gentleman was plunged into melancholy, the worse to bear from the fact that he was conscious of being comic. Trying to throw dust in his own eyes, " It is frightful how I miss Blanche," he would soliloquise at the elegiac dinner-table. But the eyes were fixed sentimentally on the place that had been Georgette's. And as the date approached for Blanche to return, and his heart sank before the necessity for resuming his capers, " It is clear," he told himself, " that the affection I entertained for that Georgette Paumelle was almost parental ! "

The fatherliness of his feelings for her, however, did not avert increased regrets at the greying moustache; and he abandoned his shaving mirror, because it magnified the lines about his nose and mouth.

Blanche, on his knee again, had plenty to tell. She described the stepfather as a " trial," and his maiden sisters as " cats." She had enjoyed herself, because Georgette and she had been together all day, but it must be hideous there for Georgette alone. " She isn't going to stick it much longer. She is miserable with them."

" How distressing that is ! " said Vauquelin. " To whom does she go? "

" Well, she has money of her own, you know— she can live where she likes."

" *Mais—Comment donc?* She cannot live by herself—une jeune fille, bien elevée ! What an idea ! Her people would never sanction it."

" I think they would be rather glad to get rid of her," said Blanche, choosing a chocolate with deliberation.

"But—but it is monstrous! To live like a bohemian, *she*! It is unheard of, terrible. Is she out of her mind? Listen, ma chérie, if her plight upsets you so violently, she can make her home with us."

"Ah, papa!" cried Blanche in ecstasy. "It is the very thing I thought of, but I was afraid it was too much to ask you."

"Now, when did I ever refuse you anything?"

"But such an enormous favour!"

"Not at all, not at all. I shall adapt myself to the arrangement well enough."

"But, papa, it might get on your nerves in time."

"Not at all, not at all. There is my study for me to retire to—I shall not see more of her than I want to."

"You promise that?"

"I can swear it."

"Oh, it will be adorable! I only wonder if I am being selfish to let you do it."

"I insist," said Vauquelin, with a noble gesture. "Say we entreat her to agree, that we shall be wounded if she declines. Say our flat is her home for as long as she will honour us—the longer, the better. *I* will write a few lines to her, too. Be tranquil, my sweet child—I do not sacrifice myself. Is it not my highest joy to indulge you?"

After many letters had been indited to her, mademoiselle Paumelle was prevailed upon to come; and after many remonstrances had been made to her, she ceased to speak of going. But for the fact that her gifts to the girl were expensive, it was as

if she were a member of the family. Blanche was
relieved to note that her papa was not driven to the
seclusion of his study often; and never did he
withdraw to it when Blanche was absent, to take
her music-lesson. As he had predicted, Vauquelin
adapted himself to the arrangement plastically.
He approved it so much, especially the tête-à-tête
during the music-lessons, that when six months
had flashed by, he resented an incident which
reminded him that it couldn't be permanent. A
monsieur Brigard, an old comrade, arrived to
advocate nothing less than that Blanche should
espouse Brigard's boy.

" My friend, I have other views for my daughter,"
replied Vauquelin firmly.

But the arrival dejected him, in the knowledge
that when Blanche should marry, Georgette would
have to go. And in their next hour alone together,
Georgette asked him what his worry was.

" Nothing. I am a little—we must all think of
the future, our children's future. A father has
responsibilities."

" À propos de—what? Am I inquisitive? "

" Do I not confide everything to you? Some
pest has made matrimonial overtures about his son.
Preposterous."

" The young man's position is not good enough? "

" Ah, his position is first rate. I say nothing
against his position."

" It is his character that displeases you? "

" No. As for that, he is steady, and not
unamiable."

" But what do you complain of ? "

Vauquelin waved his hand vaguely. " The proposal does not accord with my ideas. I have different intentions for her."

" Ah, yes, that monsieur Daudenarde ! I thought perhaps that affair had faded out."

" By no means," affirmed Vauquelin, clutching at the excuse. " Precisely. I wish her to marry monsieur Daudenarde. And that is a sound and laudable reason why I should resent being badgered by Brigard. I find such intrusions on my routine very offensive. Daudenarde's mother and I are going to have a little talk together some time or other."

" But——"

" What ? "

" You decided to have a little talk with her nine or ten months ago."

" I must avoid precipitance. In such matters a father cannot act with too much caution."

" Blanche is a darling. But there are other girls in Paris. If you desire the match, be careful you don't let him slip."

" Have no misgiving," said Vauquelin irritably. " I am quite content. Madame Daudenarde will receive a visit from me—when Blanche is older. And we shall see what we shall see."

The captivating Georgette looked thoughtful. The more so after a chat with Blanche had drawn forth the nervous confession that she " thought monsieur Daudenarde very nice."

And then, when the volatile father had banished the menace of the future from his mind, and was again basking in the sunshine of the present, what should happen but that madame Daudenarde inconsiderately broached the matter to him, instead of waiting for him to approach her.

"Dear lady, my daughter is too young," replied Vauquelin promptly.

"How, too young?" demurred madame Daudenarde. "She is one-and-twenty. I was but nineteen when I married."

"Yes," said Vauquelin, "but my sainted mother did not marry till she was thirty-two, and she always impressed upon me that it was the best age."

"Thirty-two?" cried madame Daudenarde shrilly. "Do you ask me to adjourn our conference for eleven years?"

"My honoured friend, I do not make it a hard-and-fast condition," stammered the unhappy man, struggling for coherence. "It is possible there may be something to be said against it. But your gratifying proposal is so sudden—I had not contemplated the alliance—I need time to balance my parental duties against my reverence for my mother's views."

Now, Georgette, who could put two and two together as accurately as the Minister of Finance, had not failed to remark that the interview took place privately in the study, and noted that her host was evasive when Blanche inquired why madame Daudenarde had "called at such a funny time." Feelers during the next music-lesson found him evasive also. In the days that followed, when

Blanche developed a tendency to sigh plaintively, and turned against chocolates, it grew clear to Georgette that this father must be shown the error of his ways.

"May I say that I hope that conversation with madame Daudenarde contented you?" she ventured.

"Hein?" said Vauquelin, starting.

"That the engagement will soon be announced?"

"Mon Dieu, is it not extraordinary how people seek to rob me of my child?" he moaned.

"Does that mean that nothing is arranged yet?"

"Why not leave well alone? Are we not all comfortable as we are? I have made no definite reply to madame Daudenarde — I cannot be bustled. Have you ever thought that when I part from Blanche, I shall be left here by myself?"

"Yes. It has even occurred to me that you have thought of it, too."

"Naturally. It is not strange that I should tremble at such a prospect. To be solitary is a sad thing."

"It is for your own sake, then, not hers, that you delay?"

"For the first time I find you lacking!" he broke out. "You do not seem to comprehend the workings of a father's heart."

"I have never had one."

"Don't split straws! When I lose her I shall be alone. You do not require to be a father to know that."

" You could always go to see her."

" Flûte ! "

" And your grandchildren. Respectful grand-children that clustered at your knee."

" I will not anticipate grandchildren—I am not a hundred ! " exclaimed Vauquelin angrily. " I repeat that the present conditions are entirely to my taste, and I desire to prolong them."

" It is also possible you might re-marry."

" At my age ? Who would have me ? Some ripe and ruddled widow."

" Girls, quite young, marry men much older than you."

" But not for love. Tell me, what would you put me down at ? Without flattery."

" I should call you in the prime of life."

" The friendly phrase for ' senile.' Depend upon it, people said that to Methuselah. Supposing —a man is never too old to make a fool of himself, you know—supposing, for the sake of argument, I felt a tenderness, a devotion for a girl scarcely older than Blanche : a devotion which I strove to think platonic, even while I sighed under her window, and which revived in me unsought, the emotions—all the sentiment, the throes, the absurdities—of the youth that had gone from me before I knew how divine it was. Would it—could it—is it imaginable that she might not laugh? "

" She would not laugh if she were worth it all."

" To marry me for love—a girl? To see me romantic without thinking me ridiculous—to melt to my tears, not shrink from the crows'-feet round my eyes? I wonder!"

"If you choose wisely, you will not wonder."

"In love, who *chooses?* Fate decides. What would you call 'wisely'? She should be—how old?"

"Old enough to know her mind. Young enough to attract you."

"For the rest?"

"She should have means, that you might never fear it had been yours that won her. She should have affection for your child, that she might know no jealousy of yours. She should take interest in your child's future, that, if you were wilful, she might guide you. . . . To revert to madame Daudenarde, I counsel you to write to-day that you consent."

Vauquelin stood gazing at her incredulously.

"Georgette! Georgette!" he panted. "Do you know you have given me your own portrait?"

"With my love," she told him, smiling.

F

IV

THE STATUE

IN the Square d'Iéna, which teems with little Parisians in charge of English nurses, Vera Simpson wheeled the baby-carriage to a bench on fine mornings, and exchanged patriotic sentiments with her compeers. When disparagement of France flagged, Vera Simpson occasionally observed. So as she always entered the square at the same end and nearly always chose the same bench, she observed the eccentric proceedings of a young man who took to coming every morning to stare at the statue on the opposite grass plot. After standing before it as if he were glued there, the young man would reverse one of the chairs that faced the path in an orderly line, and then sit mooning at the statue, with his back to everybody, for nearly an hour. It was, Miss Simpson surmised, a statue to a departed Frenchy. She had never approached it to ascertain what name it bore, and could see nothing about the thing to account for the fellow's taking such stock of it. Some time before he had appeared for nine days in succession, she and her circle had nicknamed him the " rum 'un."

On the tenth day, instead of the young man, a woman went to the statue, and stood before it just as stupidly and as long as the man had done. The most comical bit was that, when she turned away at last, it was seen that the statue had been making the woman cry. After that, neither of the funny pair came back to the Square d'Iéna; but as Vera Simpson chooses the same bench still, she sometimes recalls their queerness and, before her mind wanders, tries again to guess their game. This was the game that Vera Simpson tries to guess.

Gaby Dupuy was wishing that the summer were over; she was a model. Not one of the wretched models that wait at the corner of the boulevards Raspail and Montparnasse on Mondays, to crave the vote of students in academies; she went by appointment to the ateliers of the successful. But now the painters and the sculptors were all at the seaside, and her appointment book had shown no sitting for ever so long.

Gaby's qualities had never placed her among the stars of her profession. Nobody had ever said of her, as a great man said of one of the most celebrated of models, that he had only to reproduce her faithfully; still less could it be asserted that she had the genius to penetrate an artist's purport and present the pose that was eluding him. But if she had neither the beauty of a Sarah Brown, nor the intuition of a Dubosc, her face possessed a certain attractiveness, and she could achieve the expression demanded of her when it was laboriously explained.

Once upon a time her face had been more attractive still; Gaby wasn't so young as she used to be.

While the woman was regretting that her scanty provision for the dreaded summer would not allow her a more adequate menu, she received a letter. A stranger, who signed himself Jacques Launay, earnestly desired an interview. He wrote that, being unfamiliar with Paris, he had had great difficulty in ascertaining her address, and added that, as his stay in the capital was drawing to a close, he would deeply appreciate the favour of an early reply. Her eyebrows climbed as she saw that, in lieu of requiring her to betake herself to his studio, he " begged for the privilege of calling upon her at any hour that she might find con-venient." Probably, though, as a provincial, he hadn't got a studio here. Still, what deference ! he had written to her as if she were of the ancienne noblesse.

But if he hadn't a studio, where did he expect her to pose ? Did he want her to go to him in the country ? Yes, that must be it. Flûte ! Gaby didn't think it would be good enough—the end of the dead season was in sight at last, and in Paris she would often be booked for two studios a day. Nevertheless she was eager to hear what he had to say for himself. She answered that he could see her at seven o'clock the following evening at the Paradis des Artistes, round the corner. To meet him at a restaurant, she reflected, would at least ensure his asking her to have something to drink;

and as the tables would be laid, by seven o'clock, he might even spring to a meal.

The Paradis des Artistes was a small establishment where, for three francs, one found a homely dinner, inclusive of wine, and a cripple who wore a red jacket, to look like a Tzigane, and chanted to a mandoline. The " artistes " were chiefly models, and the lesser lights of a café-concert. As most of the company knew one another, and the proprietress called many of the ladies by their Christian names, and played piquet with them between midnight and 2 a.m., the tone of the restaurant was as informal as a family party. When Gaby arrived, the only person present whom she had never seen there before was a young man, who sat at a table near the door, solitary and seemingly expectant. Their gaze met, but although he looked undecided, he did not salute her. Then, as she was greeted by acquaintances, somebody cried, " Gaby, comment va ? " and the young man's head was turned again. If he was her correspondent, it was rather odd that he didn't know her when he saw her. But she gave him another opportunity. . . . He approached with marked hesitation.

" Mademoiselle Gabrielle Dupuy ? "

" Mais oui, monsieur," she said, smiling graciously. " It is monsieur Launay ? "

" Oh, mademoiselle, it is most kind of you ! " faltered the stranger. His confusion was extraordinary, considering his age, for he could not have been less than eight- or nine-and-twenty. They stood mute for some seconds. As he remained too much embarrassed to suggest her taking a seat at his table, " I hope I have not kept you waiting? " she asked, carelessly moving towards it.

They sat down now, and the waitress, whose tone was informal too, whisked over with, " And for mademoiselle Dupuy? "

" Give me a glass of madère, Louise," she said.

Still the young man seemed unable to find his tongue, and she went on :

" I am afraid this place was rather out of the way for you? But I have got into the habit of dropping in here about this time; and it is cosy and one can talk."

" Yes," he assented. He stole a timid glance at her, and looked quickly away. " Oh yes."

" Who was it who gave you my address at last, monsieur? "

" I do not know," he said awkwardly. " It was a man who heard me inquiring. I had immense trouble to find it out."

" It is not a dead secret, however."

" I suppose not—no—but I have no friends in Paris; I have never been in Paris before. And at the start I did not even know who you were."

" You did not know who I was? Oh, you had seen something I had posed for? "

" Yes, it was like that. I was anxious to find you, but I did not know your name. And I had no one to help me," he stammered; " it was enormously difficult."

" You are a painter, monsieur Launay? "

" No, mademoiselle."

" Ah, a sculptor !   That interests me still more."

" I am not a sculptor either, mademoiselle," he admitted.   " I am a composer."

" A composer ? " she echoed.   " But—but a composer does not employ models."

" No, mademoiselle, but I beg you not to think my motive impudent," exclaimed the young man, with the first touch of spontaneity that he had shown yet.

" Mysterious merely," she smiled.   Her expression offered him encouragement to elucidate the mystery, but nervousness seemed to overcome him again.   He was boring her.   She exchanged remarks across the room with a lady who wore one of the figured veils then in vogue, under which the victim of fashion appeared to have lost portions of her face.

" Going to feed, Gaby ? "

" Yes, my dear, in a minute," she answered.

She saw her correspondent regard the announcement " DINER 3 Fr."   His invitation was constrained, and her acceptance listless.

It no doubt surprised the young man to discover that the veiled lady was his guest as well; he must have wondered how it had happened.   Also it may have startled him, when he made to fill Gaby's glass from one of the little decanters that stood before them, to learn that she " did not take it " and to see a bottle labelled " Pouilly Fuissé " display itself before he could say " Why ? " for he had not heard it ordered.   He heard no order given for the second bottle that he beheld, nor for the tarte aux cerises that graced their repast—a delicacy that was not a feature of the other people's. But though these incidents may have caused him disquietude, since he was far from having an air of wealth, he manifested no objection to them. Gaby allowed that that was *gentil*. A singularly taciturn host, but an amenable one. And, briefly as he spoke, he yielded continuous attention to her prattle to the lady with the veil. It was queer that the more she prattled, the more despondent he grew. She found him piquing her curiosity.

When a bill for twenty-nine francs fifty was presented to him, after the café filtré and Egyptian cigarettes, Gaby put out her hand for it and knocked off four francs without discussion. " I don't let them make their little mistakes with friends of mine," she told him languidly, rising. " I am going home to get my coat—you can come with me." He accepted her invitation with as scant enthusiasm as she had shown for his own; and by way of a hint, forgetful of her earlier statement, she added, " This place is rotten—it's so noisy and one can't talk."

But he proved no more talkative in the street. One might almost have imagined that the task of explaining his petition for the interview was a duty that he sought to escape.

Her lodging was so close that the doorway took him aback. He followed her up the stairs submissively. She was not impatient for the coat. After lighting the lamp, she lit another of the cigarettes, and sat. The young man stood staring from the window.

" Well, chatterbox ? " she said.

He swung round with unexpected vehemence. " I know I look a hopeless idiot," he cried.

" But . . . what an idea ! " Her gesture was all surprised denial.

" I prayed to see you—I said nothing all the evening, I stand like a dummy here. I must tell you why I wrote. But—but it is not so easy as I thought it would be."

" You make me curious."

" Listen," he exclaimed. " I had had two passions in my life—music, and the poetry of Richardière ! No other poet has meant half—a tithe—so much to me as he. His work inspired me when I was a boy; if I had had the means, I would have taken the journey to Paris just to wait on the pavement and see his face when he went out. When he died—— Of course all France mourned his loss, but none but his dearest friends, I think, could have felt as I did. Well, since I have been a man I have made an opera of his *Arizath*, and I came to Paris last week because there was a prospect of its being produced. Five minutes after I had found a room at an hotel, I was asking my way to the Square d'Iéna to see the statue to him. I knew nothing about it excepting that it had been erected there—and as I approached it my heart sank : I had always pictured a statue of the man, and I saw merely a bust of him—the statue was of a woman, recalling a verse."

She nodded. " I know. Beauvais kept me posing for three hours and a half without budging, and I had a chilblain that itched like mad on the finger inside the book."

" The disappointment was keen.   I almost wished I had not come, for it had been a long walk, and I was very tired.   And then, after I had stood looking at the bust, noting how handsome he had been, and thinking of his genius, I looked down at the statue of the woman, and I felt that it would have been worth coming simply to see that.   It was so wonderful, so real !   The naturalness of the attitude, the perfection of the toilette—I had never realised that the sculptor's art could do such things; I think I looked for minutes at the slippers.   I admired the sleeves, the sweep of the gown, that seemed as if it must be soft to touch; I was amazed by a thousand trifles before my glance lingered on the face.   And after my glance lingered on the face I saw nothing else; I could not even move to look at it in profile—it held me fixed."

" It is Beauvais' masterpiece," said Gaby; " they all say it is the finest thing he has done."

" It is a masterpiece, yes.   But I was not think-ing of the sculptor and his art any more—I was thinking of the face, without remembering how it had come about.   It was as if a beautiful mind were really pondering behind that brow.   The character of the mouth and chin impressed me as if the marble had been flesh and blood; the abstracted eyes couldn't have stirred me to more reverence if they had had sight.   And while I looked at them, they seemed, by an optical illusion, to meet my own.   Not with interest; with an unconsciousness that mortified me—they seemed to gaze through my insignificance into the greatness of Richardière. I blinked, I suppose, for the next instant they had been averted. I wanted them to come back, to realise my presence. I concentrated all my will upon the effort to trick myself once more—and I could have sworn they turned. Now, too, they seemed to notice me; there was a smile in them, an ironical smile—they smiled at the presumption of my linking an immortal poet's work with mine! Insane? But I felt it, I shrank from the derision. Again I raised my head to Richardière, and for the first time I remarked that his expression was a poor acknowledgment of the figure's homage. It was consequential and impertinent. A tinge of cruelty in it, even. He had an air of sensualism, of one who held women very light. I could imagine his having said horrible things to women. He was not worthy of the look in the statue's eyes. . . .

" I went there the next day, after vowing that I would not go. The eyes discerned me sooner this time, and I contrived to fancy that their gaze was gentler. I was happy in the fancy that their gaze was gentler. When the eyes wandered from me I was humbled, and when they looked in mine I held my breath. I persuaded myself—no, I did not ' persuade myself,' the thought was born— that there was comprehension in the gaze, that my worship, though undesired, was understood. In the afternoon I had a business appointment that I had been thinking about for weeks, but instead of being excited by its nearness, I regretted that it obliged me to leave the Square d'Iéna. When I kept the appointment, the bad news that there had been a delay in the arrangements hardly troubled me—I was impatient only to be outside. Originally my plan had been to see the Louvre as soon as the business was over—now my one desire was to return to the statue. It was a delight to hasten to it; people must have thought me bound for a rendezvous, as I strode smiling through the streets. Not once did I regard the arrogance of Richardière on the pedestal, but it was only in moments that the musing figure ceased to remind me that her god was there. Though I never looked at it, an intense repugnance to the face of Richardière was in my blood—a jealousy, if you will! It possessed me while I was away—while I was reiterating that I had made my last visit to the square, knowing nevertheless that on the morrow I should yield again. The jealousy persisted when I turned the pages of my opera now, and the magic of the master's poetry was gone. I could not forget his domination of the figure—I wanted to think of the beautiful statue freed, aloof from him! "

He had left the window, and was moving restlessly about the room. Intent, her face propped by her hands, the model for the statue sat and watched him. The cigarette between her lips was out.

" The fact that there must have been a model for it was borne upon me quite suddenly. It had

the thrill of a revelation, and nearly dazed me.
This woman lived ! Somewhere in the world she
was walking, speaking ! It was as if a miracle
had happened, as if the statue had come to life.
I repeated breathlessly that it was true, but it
appeared fabulous. I had attributed emotions to
the marble figure with ease—to grasp the simple
truth of the woman's existence was inconceivably
difficult. I trembled with the marvel of it;
Pygmalion was not more stupefied than I. When
my heart left off pounding so hard, I began to
question how long it would take me to discover
who she was. I did not even know the way to set
about it. But I knew that if she was in France I
meant to find her. . . . I need not talk about the
rest."

After a silence Gaby stirred and spoke :

" It was a triumph to pose for the statue—your
story makes me very proud."

" I could not avoid telling it to you," answered
the young man drearily.

" But how you say it—as if you had done wrong !
Shall I tell you what would have been wrong?
Not to let me know. That would have been
pathetic. Mon Dieu ! it would be atrocious for a
woman to have done all that and never to hear.
And to think that at the beginning I fancied you
were—— You were so quiet while we dined."

" I was listening to you," he sighed.

" That's true. You were entitled to it by then—
you had done much to get the chance ! "

" Yes, I had done much to get the chance."

" It was beautiful of you. I mean it. Because
you have spoken earnestly, from your heart, and I
could see—I could see very well that what you
were saying was true, that you were not exaggerating to please me. Oh, I am moved, believe me, I
am really moved ! " She put out her hand to him
impulsively, and he took it, as in duty bound.
But he did not raise it to his lips. Her body
stiffened a little as the hand drooped slowly to
her lap. A shade of apprehension aged her face.
Again there was silence.

" Well ? " she murmured.

" Well ? "

" Enfin, when you sought the chance, when you
wrote to me at last, you foresaw—what ? "

" Infinitely less than you have granted, mademoiselle," he returned, with an obvious effort. " A
briefer meeting, a more formal one. I thank you
most gratefully for your patience, your kindness,
the honour you have done me."

She gave a harsh laugh. " And now you ' regret
that you must say good night ' ? "

" It is a fact that I have to see my man
again this evening," he acknowledged hurriedly,
glancing at his watch. " I had forgotten the
time."

" Yes," said the woman, " you had forgotten
the time—you had forgotten that the statue was
modelled eleven years ago. . . . So you did not
find her, after all ! You began your search too
late."

" It is not that ! " he cried, distressed.

" Ah ! " She had sprung to her feet, and stood panting. " Why lie to me? I am sorry for you, in a way—you haven't been a brute consciously."

" A brute? "

" What do you imagine you have been? A fool, you think, to yourself : I have changed, and you should have known I must have changed; it would have spared you the bother of seeking me, the disillusion when we met—there are no wrinkles creeping on the statue. Oh, it has been a fraud for you, I realise the sell! But you are not the only sufferer by your folly. A man can't talk to a woman as you have talked to me and leave her cold. He can't say, ' I felt all this for you before I saw you—now, good-bye,' and leave her proud; he can't adore her in the marble and disdain her in the flesh without her being ashamed. You have degraded me, jeered at me—you have taunted me with every blemish on my skin ! "

" It isn't that ! " he cried again. " I was a fool, I own it—a brute, if you choose to call me one— but it isn't that."

" What then? Is it my frock that alters me? I am poor, I can't afford such gowns as Beauvais put on me for the statue. Is it the way my hair is dressed? I can dress it like the statue again. The brow? You liked the brow. Well, look ! time hasn't been so rough on me there—the brow is young. And you need not be jealous of my thoughts of Richardière, for I have never read a single word he wrote. What is there lacking in me? Tell me what you miss."

" I can't tell you," he groaned. But he had started.

" You *have* told me," she said, shrinking. " I know now. My face is ignorant—the statue has more *mind* than I ! "

He no longer said, " It isn't that." He drooped before her, dumb, contrite.

After a long pause she quavered, dabbing at her eyes :

" Well, I'm not an idiot—I should improve."

" Is it an imbecile like me who could teach you ? "

" I should be content."

" Never in a single hour ! I fell in love with an ideal and went to look for it—failure was ordained. It is I who lack sense, not you."

A ghost of a smile twitched her lips. " It was all the fault of that Beauvais; he stuck an expression on me, with the clothes. I did look like that in his studio, though the chilblain was itching. But even if I made myself look like it now, it wouldn't take you in, would it ? Don't look so frightened of me, I shan't go on at you again. Poor boy, you have had a deuce of an evening ! . . . Well, I suppose you are right, failure was ordained— and it is wise to cut one's failures short. You may go. And don't flatter yourself that you have hurt me so much as I said—my vanity was stung for a minute, that's all; to-morrow I shall have forgotten all about you. . . . You can find your way downstairs ? "

He hesitated—and took an irresolute step towards her, with half-opened arms.

" Good night," she said, not moving. " Good-bye."

On the tenth day, instead of the young man, a woman went to the statue, and stood before it just as stupidly and as long as he had done. The most comical bit was that, when she turned away at last, it was seen that the statue had been making the woman cry. After that, neither of the funny pair came back to the Square d'Iéna; but as Vera Simpson chooses the same bench still, she sometimes recalls their queerness and, before her mind wanders, tries again to guess their game. This was the game that an English nursemaid tries to guess.

V

THE CELEBRITY AT HOME

Before boarding-houses in London were all called Hotels and while snobbery had advanced no further than to call them Establishments, there was one in a London square where two of the " visitors "—which is boarding-house English for " boarders "—were a girl and a young man. Irene Barton was a humble journalist, who wrote stories when she would have been wiser to go to bed, and yearned to be an admired author. Jack Humphreys was an athletic clerk, who was renouncing clerkships for Canada and foresaw himself prospering in a world of wheat. The young man and the girl used to confide their plans to each other—when they weren't saying how detestable all the other boarders were—and before the time came for him to sail they had complicated matters by falling in love.

When he had begged her to wait for him and she had explained that matrimony did not enter into her scheme of things, Miss Barton was miserable. But she did not let him guess that she was miserable, and she didn't change her mind. She had dreamed of being a celebrated novelist from the days when she wrote stories, in penny exercise books, at the nursery table, and his appeal amounted to asking her to sacrifice her aspirations and remain a nobody. She had scoffed too often at women who " ruined their careers for sickly sentiment " to be guilty of the same blunder. Still, she had had no suspicion that sentiment could lure so hard, and she viewed the women more leniently now.

She reflected that the experience of sickly sentiment at first hand should be of benefit to her fiction, but the thought failed to encourage her so much as she would have expected of it. " They learn in suffering what they teach in song," she reminded herself—and an old-fashioned instinct, which she rebuked, whispered, " But isn't it better to be happy than to teach? "

Because Jack Humphreys persisted they discussed the subject more than once. Sauntering round the garden of the square in the twilight, she expounded her philosophy to him.

" I am not," she insisted, " the least bit the kind of girl you ought to care for. It'll be five years at the very least before you can marry, and in five years' time I shall have written books, and—well, I hope I shall have done something worth while. Do you suppose I could be satisfied to give it all up? I know myself, I couldn't do it. Or, if I did do it, I should be wretched—and make you wretched too."

" But why should you give it all up? " he said miserably. " Don't you think I should be interested in it? Haven't I been interested here— have you found me so wooden? I don't know

much about it, but—— Oh, my dear, I'm so fond of
you ! Whatever interested *you* would be bound to
interest *me*. You could write novels as my wife
—I'd never put any difficulties in your way,
heaven knows I wouldn't ! "

She shook her head.

" You think all that now, but you'd know better
then. You won't want a wife to write novels—
you'll want one to bake the bread and feed the
chickens and make herself useful. You'll want the
domesticated article—and I'm an artist. I should
be an encumbrance, not a wife. Besides, I should
hate it all. Oh, I know I'm hurting you, but it's
true ! I should bore myself to death. To write,
I need to live among men and women, to live in
London, Paris, among other writers. I want to
see pictures, and hear music—real music, not
Verdi and that kind of treacle—and be in the
movement. Perhaps by the time you wanted me
to come to you I *should* be in the movement—five
years is a long while, and I'm going to work hard.
And you fancy I could turn my back on it all !
Oh, Mr. Humphreys, don't let us talk about it any
more ! "

Trying to steady his voice, the young man
asked :

" May I write to you sometimes, as a friend ? "

" I think you had better not," she said, though
her heart had jumped at the suggestion.

" I haven't any people who'd care much about
hearing from me," he pleaded ; " I shall be pretty
humped over there at the start. I'd promise

faithfully not to—er—I'd write to you just as I might write to any other chum, if I had one."

" Very well," she assented. " Write to me like that and I'll answer."

He did not write quite like that, but he suppressed two-thirds of what he wanted to say, and signed himself " Yours sincerely." Nobody could have found any definite endearment to object to in the pages. Though she checked the impulse to reply by the next mail, she replied at considerable length. She told him the latest details of the boarding-house—that Mrs. Usher was looking seriously ill because she couldn't find out why Mrs. Dunphy received so many telegrams; and that because Mrs. Kenyon's husband wasn't able to come to England yet, Mrs. Wykes was suggesting that she hadn't a husband at all. She told him that she had " had enough of these awful people " and that he was to direct his next letter elsewhere. And always his next letter was awaited more eagerly than was consistent of a young woman who was quite sure that she preferred celebrity to love.

So, although they did not write to each other more than twice or thrice a year, they were still corresponding after both had made some progress. The homestead was the man's own property at last, and the woman had had a novel published. She sent a copy of it to him, with two or three of the best reviews. It had been reviewed very highly, and if the ex-clerk had sometimes questioned whether she mightn't be exaggerating her

prospects, his doubt was banished when he read
the compliments that the critics paid her.

He grinned a little wryly in the solitude of the
homestead. Yes, it would have been a queer kind
of life here for a woman of her talent ! " I should
bore myself to death." Like a knife through him
when she said it. Of course, he had not grasped
then what the life would be. If he had thoroughly
divined—— Looking back, he wondered whether
he would have found the pluck to tackle it himself.
That first awful year, when he had ploughed a bit
of wilderness, craving in every hour for the sight
of a girl in England ! . . . Well, time worked
wonders, and his labours interested him now.
He pulled, and viewed proudly, a few heads of
the wheat he had sown with his own hands.
Jolly colour they were ! Better than a clerkship;
no more London for *him*. Irene Barton was finding
it a Tom Tiddler's ground, he supposed. Good
luck to her ! Oh, of course, she had done the
sensible thing in refusing him—and, heaven be
praised, he wasn't broken up about it any longer.
One could get over any blow.

By way of thanks for the book, he scribbled a
friendly letter, in which there was no endearment,
definite or indefinite, to object to. It implied
that her choice had been a wise one, and he congratulated her very cordially. The letter was
sincere; he felt that it would give her pleasure.
And when it reached her and she read between
the lines, the woman's heart sank, and tears crept
down her face.

He wondered mildly why he didn't hear from her any more.

The novel that the papers praised so warmly had enriched her by the sum of ten pounds; and when she was five years older than she had been on the day she said good-bye to him, she was writing in a boarding-house much like the one where he had met her. She remembered wistfully that within five years she had foreseen herself rejoicing in Upper Bohemia.

She wrote well. She did not think as well as she wrote, of course—her horizon was clouded by myths, like those that have it that Scots are all skinflints, and Jews are all rogues—but her work had beauty; and critics saw it, and she made a reputation. But the general public did not see it, or, seeing the beauty, were a Channel's width from perceiving that it was beautiful, so she did not make money. And without money she found a literary reputation was less ecstatic than she had presumed. It did not mean congenial society, because she could not afford to join the clubs where congenial society might be supposed to exist. It did not mean concerts, or picture-galleries, or less physical discomfort, or a breath of sea air when she was sick for it; it did not mean a single amelioration of her life's asperities, because Press notices were not to be tendered in lieu of cash. Even those who lauded her fiction remained strangers to her. Only for a few weeks after each book was issued, she read, in her boarding-house

attic, that she was a " distinguished novelist,"
and then she was again ignored.

And meanwhile her youth was fading, and her
eyes were dimming, and she looked in the glass
and mourned. In the emptiness of her " distinction " she longed for laughter and a home.
Desperate at last, she did join a club of professional
women; but nominal as the fees were, considering
the splendour of the place, it was an annual effort
for her to pay the subscription. And she did not
go there often enough to make any intimate
friends, because she was generally too tired.

And every year she grew more tired still.

When she had been growing tired for sixteen
years she was in a dreary lodging, in a dingy street,
toiling at a novel, between the fashion articles by
which she earned her daily bread. Mr. Humphreys,
in easy circumstances by this time, was in London
too, though when memories awoke in her she
pictured him in Manitoba. He was indulging in
a trip, and had been in England three weeks.
One afternoon, in the hall of the new and expensive
hotel, he picked up a book and came upon her
name among the publisher's advertisements. It
was an advertisement of one of her shattered hopes,
but Mr. Humphreys didn't know that—he merely
saw her referred to as a " distinguished novelist."
She was, at the moment, trudging from a modiste's
to a milliner's, to gather something to say in her
inevitable article. It was raining, and she had a
headache, and she would have to hammer out a

sprightly column about Paris models before she could lie down. His holiday was proving rather dull, and he wondered idly whether it would be a foolish impulse to recall himself to such a prominent woman.

His formal note, re-directed by the publisher's clerk, and re-directed again, reached her some days later. " If you have not quite forgotten our old friendship, I should be glad of an opportunity to call and congratulate you on your triumphs." She read that line many times. Her face was white, and her eyes were wide. She looked again at the name of the expensive hotel, and stared at the sordid parlour in which she sat—the pitiable parlour with its atrocious oleographs on drab walls, and two mottled vases, from the tea-grocer's, on the dirty mantelpiece. He would be " glad to congratulate her " !

She remembered the unaffected cheeriness of the previous congratulations, the letter that had shown her his love was dead. She had fancied that nothing could hurt more deeply than that letter, but she had been wrong—to expose her mistake to him would be bitterer still. The humiliation of it, the punishment ! All the arrogance of her rejection, all the boasts of her girlhood thronged back upon her tauntingly. God ! if she could have seen ahead—if only she could have her life again.

She debated her reply. To say that she was leaving town would sound ungracious. The alternative was to receive him at the club. Almost for the first time she was devoutly thankful to be a member—the club would spare her the ignominy of revealing her parlour; the stationery would avert the need for betraying her address.

On the imposing stationery she wrote that she would be " pleased to see him here on either Wednesday or Thursday next." Her clothes, she supposed, wouldn't give her away, as he was a man.

Was he married? There was no hint of a wife in his letter. How much changed would she find him? Would the change in herself shock him greatly? There were women as old as she who were still spoken of as " young," but their lives had run on smoother lines than hers—and when he saw her last she had been twenty-two and sanguine. It seemed to her that he would meet a stranger. She trembled in the club on Wednesday afternoon, and began to hope that his choice would fall on " Thursday."

She was told that he had come. She rose with an effort. A big man, with greying hair, approached her uncertainly. She smiled with stiff lips. " Mr. Humphreys," she faltered. And a voice that she didn't remember, a new deep voice that wasn't like Jack's at all, was saying, " Why, Miss Barton! This is very kind of you."

" How d'ye do? So glad to see you again," she murmured. " Let—let us go and sit down." Her heart was thumping, and she felt a little deaf. " So—er—— Well, how does London look to you after such a long time? Are you home for good? "

" No, about a couple of months. My home is on the other side now. Well, this is a real pleasure ! I never expected—I was rather nervous about writing, but——"

" It would have been too bad if you hadn't," she said.

" Well, I thought I'd take my chance. Er— yes, London looks rather different. I managed to get lost in it the other day; I had to find a taxi to take me back. No taxis when I was here before ! "

" You take tea ? "

The alcove was very comfortable, and the long room was exquisite in all its tones. The beauty of the carpet, she felt, more than repaid her for that annual effort. And how deferential was the service !

" A fine place," said Mr. Humphreys admiringly.

" Yes, it's rather decent," she drawled ; " they do one very well here. A club is one of the necessaries of life."

" I suppose so." He was remembering the way her tea had been served in the boarding-house. " Wealth buys more in the old country than over there—you get more for your money than I do."

" Do you have to rough it very badly ? " Her tone was gentler. " Are you still in the same place ? "

" Well, I haven't known I was roughing it of recent years, but I don't see luxury like this in Manitoba. Not bad. And I've got a gramophone. Pretty rotten records, I'm afraid. Verdi is about the most classical of them."

" Isn't it lovely, how Verdi reminds one ? " she

said. " If I hear Verdi, I'm about ten years old
again, and—it's funny—I'm always in the same
bow window, and it's always a summer's afternoon,
though I suppose the organs used to come in the
winter, too. Just as, if I hear that hymn with
' pilgrims of the night ' in it, it's always the nursery,
and the gas over the mantelpiece is lighted. Verdi
gives me my childhood back. I hope to hear
Verdi in heaven. You've nothing very dreadful
to complain of, then ? You aren't sorry you went ? "

" Well, no—I'm glad I went. It has panned
out all right. It has been a funny thing to walk
down the Strand again and remember that the
last time I was in it I was short of sixpences. The
other day I looked in at the office where I used to
clerk. Two of the boys I had known were there
still—grown round-shouldered and pigeon-chested.
I suppose they've had a rise of about fifty pounds
a year in the meantime. They came round to
dinner at the hotel last night, and it made me
melancholy to hear them talk. I used to want
them to chuck the office and go out to Canada
with me—they'd got the stamina once—but they
hadn't got the grit. Now it's too late. . . . You
know, it's capital to see you flourishing like this !
You're about the only survivor of the old days
that it hasn't given me the hump to meet. You
always *were* sure you'd get on, weren't you ? "

" I was," she said. " Yes, I used to say so."

" Do you remember the people in that house ?
And how we used to groan about the extras in the
bills ? "

" It was a bad time for us both," she stammered.

" But it's good to look back on now it's over. Helps one to appreciate. When you're feeling dull now, you can drive round here and have a chat with a friend, and say, ' Well, it used to be much worse—I used to be poor.' Isn't that so ? "

She nodded helplessly. Her mind was strained to find another subject.

" I wish *you'd* come round to dinner with me one evening, if you've nothing better to do ? "

" I'm not going out very much just now," she demurred. " I——"

" It'd be a charity, I'm all alone, and—by the way, I don't know if ' Miss Barton ' is just your literary name now ? If there is a lucky man, I hope he will give me the pleasure, too ? "

" No, I'm not married," she said.

" Like me, you've been too busy. You know, I really think our victories should be fêted. It'd be friendly of you to come. You can find one evening free before I go back ? "

" I suppose," she said, trying to laugh, " I'm not so full of engagements that I can't do that ! "

And, though neither of them had foreseen the invitation, she was pledged to dine with him. Heavily she reflected that, when the dinner finished, she would be obliged to ask him to send for a taxi and that it would probably cost her a half-crown.

She went by train. That her solitary evening gown was wrong, having been bought three years since, did not worry her, though as " Lady

Veronica," in her *The Autocrat at the Toilet-Table* column, she wrote of things being " hopelessly last season's " when their vogue had been declining for a week; but she was embarrassed by her lack of evening shoes. At the table she bore herself bravely, supported by the knowledge that the epoch of her sleeves was unsuspected by him, but when she rose she found it difficult to conceal her feet.

Yet, if it had not been that the shame of failure poisoned each mouthful that she took, the evening would have had its fascination. When she led him to speak of his early blunders on the homestead, while he told her how he had shrunk dismayed from the first bleak sight of that patch of prairie, she forgot she was pretending, and forgot to feel abased. In moments she even forgot to feel old. The story of his struggles bore her back. As she heard these things, the greying man became to her again the boy that had loved her—and as the woman leant listening, the man caught glimpses of the girl that she had been.

His trip was proving queerly unlike his forecast of it on the farm. When he packed his bags he had had no idea of seeing her, but he had looked for emotions that he hadn't obtained. The strangeness of sauntering on the London pavements as a prosperous man had been less exhilarating than his anticipation of it. To drive to a fashionable tailor's and order clothes had failed to induce a burst of high spirits, though on the way he had laudably reminded himself that once it would have been the day of his life. He was, in fact, feeling solitary, and to loll in stalls at the theatres, instead of being jammed in the pit, would have seemed livelier to him if he had had a companion. In the circumstances, it was not astonishing that he proposed to take Irene Barton to the theatre a night or two later—and as he insisted a good deal, she compromised with a matinée.

Somehow or other he was having tea with her, at the club again, the day afterwards. And on the day after that, there was something else.

They had always found much to say to each other in the old days—they found much to say now, when the constraint wore off. The man told himself that he felt a calm friendship for the woman whom he had once wanted for his wife. And the woman told herself that, since he would soon be gone, she'd snatch happy hours with the man she loved while he was here. Her philosophy had changed since she expounded it in the garden of the square.

And then—the claims of *The Autocrat at the Toilet-Table* had compelled her to break an appointment—it manifested itself to Mr. Humphreys that his feelings were not so calm as he had thought. Irritable in the hotel hall, he perceived that this " friendship " threatened his holiday with a disastrous end. He wanted no second experience of fevering in Canada for a face in England. Grimly he decided that the acquaintance must be dropped. If it came to that, why remain in England any longer? It was time for him to go.

On the morrow, in another charming corner of
the familiar club, he told her his intention, and she
tried to disguise how much it startled her. When
she had " hoped that he hadn't received bad news "
and he had said briefly that he hadn't, there was a
pause. In his endeavour to be casual he had been
curt, and both were conscious of it. He wondered
if he had hurt her. Perhaps he should have offered
an excuse for his sudden leave-taking? He began
to invent one—and she politely dismissed it. He
was certain now that he had hurt her. After all,
why not be candid?

He leant forward, and spoke in a lowered
tone :

" Do you know why I'm going? I'm going
because, if I stopped, I should make a fool of
myself again."

The cup in her hand jerked. She felt suffocating,
voiceless. Not a word came from her.

" I'm remembering that discretion is the better
part of valour, Miss Barton."

" How do you mean? " she faltered.

" I'm running away in time. You see, I—I
made a mistake : I reckoned you wouldn't be
dangerous to me any more, and I was wrong. . . .
So you won't think me ungrateful for going, will
you? You've given me some very happy hours;
I don't want you to think I didn't appreciate them.
But I appreciate, too, the fact that you're a successful woman and that I've even less to hope for now
than I had before. I went through hell about
you once, dear—I couldn't stick it twice."

Her hand was passed across her eyes, and she trailed it on her skirt.

" Are you running away from—from my success ? If I cared for you, do you think my success would matter ? "

" Do you care for me ? " His voice shook, like hers. He hated the chattering groups about them, as he bent conventionally over the tea-table. " Do you mean you could give your position up to be my wife ? "

She rose. Her lips twitched before her answer came. It came in a whisper :

" You've never seen my rooms. Will you drive me there ? "

And on the way she was very quiet.

The taxi stopped. In a dingy street she took a latchkey from her pocket, and opened a door, from which a milk-can hung. Perplexed, he followed. She led him to a parlour—a pitiable parlour, with atrocious oleographs on drab walls, and two mottled vases on a dirty mantelpiece.

" This," she said dryly, " is where I live. You see the celebrity at home."

He tried to take her to him, and she drew swiftly back.

" I have failed," she cried; " no one has read my books; I'm as poor as when you knew me first. I've spent years in holes like this ! I've shammed to you because I was ashamed. My talk of people I know, of places I go to has been lies—I know no one, I go nowhere. I refused to marry you, when I was a girl, because I didn't think it good enough

H

for me; before you stoop to ask me again, go away and think whether it's good enough for *you*. I've lost my hopes, my youth, my looks—you'd be giving me everything, and I should bring you nothing in return!"

His arms were quick now, and they held her fast. "Nothing?" he demanded. His eyes challenged her. "Nothing, Irene?"

"Oh, my dearest," she wept, smiling, "if my love's enough——?"

VI

PICQ PLAYS THE HERO

WHEN he had made his choice of a career, when in spite of remonstrances he had become an actor, his father had felt disgraced. His father was the hatter in the rue de la Paroisse. The shop was not prosperous—in Ville-Nogent people made their hats last a long while—but it was at least a shop, and the old man wished his son to be respectable. This, you see, was France. The little French hatter had not heard that, across the Channel, the scions of noble houses turned actors, and he would not have believed it if he had been told.

Once, the son of a little French tradesman humiliated his father by going on the stage and became the admiration of the world; but this tradesman's son did not distinguish himself like that. Indeed, he did not distinguish himself at all. Many years later the hatter patted the artist's hand, and said feebly : " After I am gone, take a hat, my poor Olivier. Heaven knows thou needest one ! " A hat, and his blessing were well-nigh all he had to give by this time.

In his youthful dreams—day-dreams behind the counter—Olivier Picq had seen himself a leading man in Paris, making impassioned love in the

limelight to famous actresses. His engagements
had proved so different from his dreams that not
once had he attained to the hero's part, even in the
least significant of provincial holes. No manager
could be induced to regard him as a hero. By
slow degrees he had ceased to expect it. By still
slower degrees he ceased to expect even parts of
prominence. He was the fatuous valet, who came
on, with the laughing chambermaid, to explain
what the characters that mattered had been doing
between the acts; he was the gaby that made
inane remarks, in order that the low comedian
might reply with something funny; he was the
moody defaulter that committed suicide early in
the piece—and he changed his wig (alas! not his
voice) to become the uninteresting figure that
broke the tragic tidings to the widow.

"Ah," says the reader, "he wasn't clever.
That's why he didn't get on."

Well, it is not pretended that Picq had genius;
for such parts as fell to him he had not even marked
ability. But the truth is, that in the rôle of
romantic hero, which he had not had a chance to
play, he would have been good. The laughing
chambermaid used to say he would have been
splendid. Often they grieved over the bad luck
that had attended him, as they reviewed the years
of struggle, hand in hand. He had married the
chambermaid.

"Oh, I can guess the end of this story already!"
says the reader. "He became a leading man in
Paris, after all."

So he did, madam. But not quite so felicitously as you may think. Picq, dizzied by the sudden transformation, was promoted to be the hero—a gallant, dashing boy—in a revival on a Paris stage, one winter when he was subject to lumbago, and fifty-eight years old. You see, most of the actors of military age that still lived were either in the line or the hospitals, while many of the popular actresses were nursing. A manager who had the temerity to cast a play now was in no position to be fastidious, and playgoers were indulgent. They accepted the elderly man as the gallant boy. He was applauded. And while he declaimed bombast across the footlights—those turgid love appeals to which he had aspired, behind the counter, forty years ago—it was with a heart torn with anxiety for his own boy, who was in the trenches.

When Jean had slept as a baby, the utility actor and the chambermaid had sat by the cradle and talked in low tones of the fine things he was to do when he grew up. Not on the stage—both had outlived its glamour; he was to be an advocate. " It is so refined, dearest," said the chambermaid. " And there is money in it, my love," agreed the father. And for half a lifetime unflinchingly they had scraped and hoarded, to realise that ambition for him. Their salaries were not vast, and there were numerous vacations in which there was no salary at all; often the sum that they had garnered during one tour would melt before the next; but every hundred francs that they could stick to looked a milestone on the journey. Only one annual extravagance did they allow themselves. On Jean's birthday it was Picq's custom to take home a bottle of cheap champagne. The dinner might be meagre, the vacation might be long, but on Jean's birthday they must be joyous. And in a shabby lodging-house bedroom—a parlour was beyond the means of poor players who pinched to make their son an advocate—the pair would festively clink glasses to his future.

" We have not been unhappy together all these years, Nanette, my little wife, though you did throw yourself away in marrying me, hein? " Picq would say tenderly, embracing her. And Nanette, who still looked almost as young sometimes as she had looked at the wedding breakfast —at any rate, Picq thought so—would answer, with a catch in her voice : " Sweetheart, I have thanked the good God on my knees every night for that ' throwing myself away.' "

" All the same, it is possible that, without me, you would have got on far better—even have made a name."

" Silly ! It is more likely *I* who have held *you* back; perhaps alone you would have gone to the top. Ah, no, I cannot bear to think it; I cannot bear to think I have been a hindrance to you ! "

Then Picq, denying it vigorously, would cry : " But a fig for the stage ! Ma foi, have we not each other, and our Jean? It is wealth enough. I tell you he is going to be a famous man one day, our Jean—he has the brow."

By rare good fortune, when he was old enough
to have ideas of his own on the subject of a career,
Jean had not opposed their plan; he did not, as
might easily have been the case, inherit a craving
to be the hero. He had long been a student in
Paris, and they were playing in a rural district
remote from him on the day of the mobilisation.
Never while life lasted would they forget that day
—that beating on a tocsin, and the glare of a blue
sky that turned suddenly black to them; the
deathly silence that spread; and then the shrill
voice of a child, the first to speak—" *C'est la
guerre !* " The shaking of their limbs held the
father and mother apart; only their gaze rushed
to each other. " Jean ! " she had moaned.

And Jean fought for France still, and already it
seemed to them that the war was eternal. Twice
—on two anniversaries since that terrible Saturday
—they had raised trembling glasses to a photograph on the wall and pretended to be gay, and a
third anniversary was approaching. " Be confident, be brave," he wrote to them; " we are
going to win." But the thoughts that crowded on
his little mother, in the dark, after she went to bed
kept her awake for hours; and marking the change
that the war had wrought in her, Picq's misgivings
for his wife were sometimes hardly less acute than
his anxieties for his boy. The laughing chambermaid, who had retained girlishness of disposition
for two decades after girlhood was past, seemed to
him all at once middle-aged. Ever the first formerly to propose trudging a long distance to save a

tram fare, she was now fatigued after an hour's stroll. By the time they came to Paris, too, she was subject to spells of some internal trouble, which the doctor had failed to banish permanently. There could be no question of her seeking an engagement.

" It *is* a shame, when the double salary would have been so nice," she repined, one evening. The trouble had recurred, and a new doctor had been no more definite than his predecessor. " We might have lived on my money, and put the whole of yours aside every week. It *is* a shame that you should have an invalid for a wife."

" An invalid ! " laughed Picq, affecting great amusement. " Now, is not that absurd ? To hear you talk, one would imagine it was some terrible malady, instead of a little derangement of the system that will pass and be forgotten. Very likely you will be in a show again before Jean's birthday. And it shall be a good part, also, parbleu ! There are not so many stars available to-day that they can afford to put on an artist like you to flick the furniture with a feather-brush. Listen, Nanette, my best beloved, if it were anything serious that you had the matter with you, it would not right itself as it does from time to time—it would be always the same. The fact that you are sometimes as well as ever shows that it is nothing organic. Have not both doctors said so ? Did not the other man tell us so again and again ? "

She nodded, forcing a smile. Her smile was

girlish still, and somehow it looked to him strangely poignant on her altered face. His gaze was blurred, as he muffled himself in his shabby cloak, and set forth through the sleet, to be the dashing hero. A child came towards him, calling papers, and he thought, " If only the news were that Germany sued for peace ! That would be the best medicine for her."

And on the morning before the birthday she was *not* " in a show again "; she was feeling so much worse that she clung to Picq, alarmed. Picq was alarmed, too, though he tried to hide it.

" Look here, I tell you what ! " he exclaimed, in the most confident tone that he could summon. " We are going to call in a big man and get you cured without any more delay ! That's what we're going to do. This chap is too slow for me. I dare say his medicines might do the trick eventually, but it does not suit me to wait so long. No, it does not suit me. I am not going to see you worried like this while he potters about as if time were no object. We shall call in a big man and put an end to the nuisance at once. I wish to heaven I had done it before. I am going now. I am going to the chap's house to tell him plainly I am not content."

" Mais non, mais non ! " demurred Nanette piteously. " It would cost such a lot, chéri— what are you thinking about ? I shall get all right without that. You mustn't take any notice of me; I am a coward—I have never been used to feeling ill, you see—but I shall get all right without that."

" I care nothing what it costs. That is my
intention," declared Picq. " And it will not cost
such a great sum either. Anyhow, whether it is
forty francs or five hundred, my mind is made up.
I am going to him this moment to tell him I want
the highest authority in Paris. Now, be tranquil,
mignonne. Try to sleep. We have chosen the
shortest course at last—we were bien bêtes not
to take it at the start—and in a week at the outside
you will be yourself again."

Never in her life had Nanette contemplated
spending forty francs all at once on a physician.
She knew she would be unable to sleep for the
awfulness of such expense. But, if his prescription
cured her promptly and she could earn a salary
again soon——

" What a weight I have become to thee, my
little husband ! " she faltered, stroking his hand.

" Hush ! Thou *wilt* sleep while I am away,
pauvrette ? " asked Picq tenderly.

She closed her eyes, smiling—to lie and grieve
over the " weight she had become to him " when
he had gone; and Picq went apace to the doctor's.

When the motive for the inopportune call was
explained, the doctor evidently resented the
suggestion that his own treatment of the patient
could be bettered.

" Another opinion, monsieur? Parfaitement—
if you desire it." His shrug was eloquent. " But
your wife has only to continue with the medicine
I have prescribed——"

" She has continued," stammered Picq; " she

has continued. There it is—she has continued for a long time. I grow anxious. No doubt it is unreasonable of me, but——" Truth to tell, the veteran of the boards, who faced a crowded auditorium without a tremor, found himself nervous in the room of the dignified practitioner.

" One must not expect miracles. I am not a magician. In such cases——"

" Mais enfin, another opinion would ease my mind. If you would do me the great kindness to indicate a specialist, monsieur—the best? Such a one as you would recommend if it were—I do not know what it *could* be, I; but such a one as you would recommend if you feared something grave? I should be thankful. I know nothing of these things. If you would be so very kind as to communicate with someone for me——" He withdrew, after five minutes, clumsily, relieved to be able to tell Nanette that, with luck, they might receive a visit from a specialist on the morrow.

" And his charge—how much? " panted Nanette, who feared that such celerity might cost more still.

When the specialist had been, on the morrow—when Picq had closed the street door after him, and stumbled up the stairs, in his hurry to rejoin Nanette, and sat down on the bed, with his cheek resting against hers—they did not speak for some seconds.

" Well, well," he brought forth at last, " after all, it is not so bad, what? It is a shock, of course

—I own it is a shock; but really, when one comes
to think it over——"

She moaned—a child afraid.

" Don't—*don't!*   An operation ! "

" Yes, yes, it is a shock; we were hoping for an
easy cure.   But when all is said, we have learnt
there *is* a cure.   If he had told us there was nothing
to be done?   There *is* a cure !   And you will feel
nothing, mignonne—you will feel no pain at all.
And afterwards, when you lie there at peace—so
comfortable in the knowledge that all the misery
is over—I shall come every day and bring you
flowers.   And every day I shall find you brighter
and stronger.   Upon my word, I would not mind
making a bet that, in looking back at it, you
remember it as a happy time."

Big tears were on her frightened face.

" And it is Jean's birthday," she wailed.

" Yes, it is unfortunate.   It cannot be helped.
Well, we shall have our fête when you come home
instead, and—listen, listen !   We will drink his
health at a restaurant—we will make up for the
delay.   To the devil with the cost !   When you
come home cured, we will have a swagger supper
out, to celebrate the double event.   Nanette—it
is useless to expostulate—I register a vow that this
time we will squander a couple of louis on a supper
on the Boulevard.   And you shall put on your
pink silk dress ! "

" Petit bonhomme, wilt thou do me a favour? "
she whimpered.

" Now thou art going to say something foolish."

" No; we will have that supper on the Boulevard. After the awful expense I shall have been, two louis more or less—— But let us fête Jean the same as usual to-night. We must. We've never missed doing it once since he was a baby; I couldn't bear to let the day go by without our doing that. Think of the danger he is in. Get champagne as you always do. If it would be bad for me, I won't take any; but get it! My illness mustn't spoil the birthday altogether. Get it, and we'll forget about me for an hour. Chéri, I shall go into the hospital braver in the morning for having had our fête."

" Agreed, agreed," said Picq chokingly. " But it will be a poor treat to me, if I am to drink it alone. I shall ask if you may take a sip."

He rang up the specialist, to inquire, on the way to the theatre in the evening. " It is our boy's birthday, monsieur," he pleaded—" our boy who is in the war. You see, it is his birthday!"

" One glass of champagne? Yes. It will do no harm," said the authoritative voice. " But no excitement, you understand. And no solid food. To-morrow and the next day they will see to her diet—and the day after that, we shall operate."

That word " operate," booming from the receiver, struck horror to Picq afresh. He marvelled that anyone could be capable of uttering it so cheerfully, as he went out into the streets again. A child came towards him, calling papers, and he sighed, " If they but announced that Germany sued for peace ! She would not be thinking so much about the operation then."

During the performance, the bottle of paltry wine stood among the articles of make-up on the table of his dressing-room; and in his wait in the last act, he sat staring at it, and thinking of the days when his boy in the 120ième Régiment Terri-torial had been a tiny child, and the wife who was so ill had been all sunshine and laughter. It had not been withheld from him, on the doorstep, in the morning, that the operation would be a serious one, and he felt sick in contemplating the next three days' suspense. How would Nanette con-trive to bear it, he wondered, away from him, among strangers in a hospital? When the fearful moment came for her to be carried from the ward to the operating table——! Cold sweat burst out on him. As he sat huddled there, in the garish dressing-room, Picq prayed to Heaven to give her courage. His chin was sunk on his chest; he rocked to and fro.

There was a sudden rap at the door.

" Entrez ! " said Picq, and somebody brought him a telegram.

He read : " I have the pain of informing you of the death on the field of honour of your son Jean Picq." It was from the War Office.

" Better hurry up, Picq—you haven't too long ! " called a colleague, carelessly, looking in. " Good God ! " And he sprang towards him.

Picq staggered, from his colleague's arms, up the crazy staircase to the wings—and straightened his back to be dashing. He entered upon the scene in time. And he delivered his lines, and struck his attitudes, and paused, by force of habit, when a round of applause was due. At the climax of a tirade, when he took a step back and mechanically raised his gaze to the first circle, nobody would have supposed that, with his mind's eye he looked, through the tier of faces, on the mangled body of his son.

The curtain fell again. The play was over, and he tottered back to the room. The bottle of champagne on the dressing-table, among the litter of make-up, was the first thing he noticed. " My wife ! " gasped Picq, and broke down. He was shaken by sobs.

Some of the players had followed. Sympathy surrounded him.

" I see her face when I tell her—I see her face ! How to keep it from her ? To-night she mustn't know—it would kill her; but to keep it from her for weeks till she has recovered—is it possible? "

" Poor chap ! Be brave. Time——" They mumbled useless words.

" To have to pretend to her every time I go, for weeks, perhaps months ! And then, when she is so happy at being well again, to have to strike her down with the blow ! Ah, I know I am not the only father to lose his son—she is not the only mother, but——"

" You don't think it might be best to break it to her now? " someone suggested.

He shook his head impatiently, the throbbing

head from which the jeune premier's curls were not removed yet.

" It would be murder. I am warned she is to avoid excitement. And this evening, when she tries to be bright, to go in and say, ' He is killed ' ! I mustn't tell her till she is well—quite, quite well. I must keep her cheerful; I must be in good spirits, but—I haven't the courage to go home."

It was the truth : he had not the courage to go home.

" She is waiting for me—I must make haste to change," he faltered more than once; but even when he had " changed " at last, his soul cowered before the thought of the ordeal, and he lingered nerveless in the chair.

" She is waiting for me—I must go," he kept repeating while the lights in the theatre went out. " I must go," he said again, and rose. They had called a cab for him, and his legs felt so unreliable that he offered no protest, though a cab seemed a terrible extravagance. Yes, he would take one; it was certain he could not walk fast enough to make up for the delay, and Nanette mustn't be allowed to grow anxious. He lay back in the cab dizzily, a hand round the neck of the bottle on his knees. " In good spirits—in good spirits ! " he cautioned himself. " But her instinct is so strong. If she suspects ? " On the rattling course, imagination wrung him with the moment of her suspicion —the horror in her dilating eyes, the impuissance of his agony. . . . " Dead ! " He perceived with a shock that he had not understood that Jean was

dead—that he still did not understand. "Dead."
Jean, who seemed so vividly alive, was only a
memory. His eagerness, his laughter, his allusions,
all the intimate realities that represented Jean had
been blown out. It was inconceivable; his mind
would not grasp it. Where, then, did comprehension lie, that he was stricken? . . . The cab
startled him by stopping.

As he had said, she was trying to be bright.
She had not cast her fears aside, but she meant to
hide them. She welcomed him with a smile.
"Champagne *and* a cab? What next?"

"Yes, what do you think of it? I was in a
hurry to get back. How has it been with you,
chérie—has the evening seemed very long? Well,
there is good news—you may have a glass."

"He was sure?"

"He said 'Yes' at once. Oh, I wouldn't have
tried to persuade him—that would have been folly.
I told him the reason, but I did not try to persuade
him."

"How tired you look! How did it go?"

"It was a good audience—what there was of it.
Three calls after the third act. What an appetite
I've got—and what a thirst! I can't wait to take
my boots off. The spread attracts me. What?
I declare I see my favourite sausage!"

"I couldn't go out for any flowers this year, and
I forgot to remind you," she said. "But you'll
find enough to eat."

"And you—what is there for *you?* Let me
put the pillow behind you, mignonne. And now

I

to open the bottle! I am not an expert at the game, but—ah! it is coming. Prepare yourself for the bang. . . . Tiens, it is of a gentle disposition. But no doubt it will taste just as good. Sapristi, how it sparkles!"

He bore a glassful to her side, and their gaze turned together to the likeness on the wall.

"Well, little wife, the usual toast. To our boy, our darling Jean! May God bless him."

"May God bless him," breathed the mother. They looked at the photograph silently for a moment. "I wonder if he is thinking of us?" she murmured. "Perhaps he is fancying us like this?"

"I venture to say so," replied Picq. "He knows we should never forget his birthday; he knows that."

"If—he is alive," she said in a whisper.

"Ah, why should we doubt it?" His arm encouraged her. "How often we have alarmed ourselves! And always he *was* alive. Take another sip, mignonne. It is a sound wine, hein? I should not be surprised if on the Boulevard they charge fifteen francs for such a wine."

"You must go and sit down now and have your supper."

"Not for a minute or two. The bouquet is so excellent I can't take my nose out of the glass. And I think I am more thirsty than hungry, after all."

"Petit bonhomme, petit bonhomme," she faltered pitifully.

"And why 'petit bonhomme' like that—what are you making so much of me about?"

" Do you think I am blind? Do you suppose you can hide it from me? Your hands tremble and your eyes are red. As soon as you came in I saw. You have been tormenting yourself about the operation all the evening."

" Mais non, mais non! If I worry, it is not about the operation, because it is a simple thing, though it sounds so big to *us*. They tell me it is an everyday affair, like having out a tooth; that was his very expression : ' Monsieur, it is no more dangerous than having out a tooth.' I worry, if I worry at all, in thinking that you are frightened. If I could only make you believe that there is nothing to be frightened of ! "

" I know I am a coward. I told you so. It is from *you* that he gets his courage."

" What an illusion ! A fine fire-eater *I* am ! Old stick-in-the-mud ! "

" Ah, yes. I'm ashamed. When I think of what he is going through—how splendidly he bears it ! And here am I, afraid of everything. He has no heroine for a mother."

" I forbid thee to say it. He knows it is not true."

" He loves me just the same. Don't you, Jean —you don't love your little mother any less? " The photograph hung too high for her. " Take it down," she pleaded. " If I could change places with thee, my son ! I would find the courage for that, though I died of terror in the first hour. Ah, my little baby, my little baby ! And I was so glad he was a boy ! "

" You are not to upset yourself," quavered Picq.
" I cannot stand it. Will you be sorry he was a
boy when he gets the Croix de Guerre? I make
you a bet they give him that at the very least. I
see you polishing it all day. Pick up your glass.
To tell the truth, I have a strong presentiment, and
I am not given to foolish fancies, that he comes
home ' Captain.' What triumph for us—hale and
hearty and a captain. Imagine it. At his age!
Nanette, pick up your glass. We will paint the
town red that night, and you will say you were
' always sure of it.' When I chaff you about your
tremors you will declare you never had any.
Mind you, I am putting it down very low; it is
quite on the cards that he becomes ' Colonel.'
Nanette, I entreat thee, pick up thy glass! Again
a toast. Good luck, my son! We drink to your
future. A bumper to our next merry meeting! "

That toast reverberated to Picq when she lay
sleeping and Picq was sleepless. But, at any rate,
she had no suspicion so far.

She remained without suspicion when he visited
her at the hospital, during the following week, but
always she remained a prey to fear. Not for
herself now—they said the operation had been
successful; it was the thought of Jean's peril that
haunted her. As she was wakened in the early
morning, the burden of dread rolled upon her.
Through the long monotonous day her mind was
in the blood-soaked line more often than in the ward.
They hinted to Picq that her anxiety was detri-
mental, and he tried to reason with her once; but

it seemed to do more harm than good, for she burst out, " If he should be killed ! " and wrung her hands on the quilt. " He has everything before him, he's so fond of life. If he should be killed ! "

" He will not be killed. Is not my love for him as great as yours? And you see I am confident. I swear to you I am confident ! I implore you, don't dwell on these thoughts. Make haste and get well." And again he asked himself, " How am I to break it to her when she *is* well? "

Then there was a morning when they sent him away for a while, stupefied by the announcement that never would she be well. " The conditions had changed "; he must be " prepared for the worst." She, too, had been prepared, before he was admitted. He had foreseen her speechless with fright; but, strange to say, the " coward " who had been so timorous of an operation, had spoken of her approaching death quite calmly. Her terror for Jean it was, increasingly her terror for Jean, that tortured her last hours. " Petit bonhomme, it is like being on the rack," she had gasped. " If only I were sure he would be spared ! "

" God of heaven, it is ' like being on the rack ' for her," shuddered Picq, sobbing in the street; " it is for her ' like being on the rack ' ! And there is nothing I can do."

And a child came towards him, calling papers.

It was with the connivance of the nurses that he brought joy and thanksgiving to her heart during the hours that remained to her. He pretended to her that Germany sued for peace. If he was condemned to affect the tones of hysterical rejoicing, he had no need to counterfeit the tears. Tears were rolling down his cheeks, as he feigned to fight for mastery of a whirlwind of exultance, and panted to her that the war was won.

"I return with good news—the greatest; but I implore thee, keep still—they forbid thee to sit up. Nanette, my loved one, our boy is safe. The danger is all over—he will soon be home. The Boches are beaten. I rush back to tell thee. They cave in. Paris has gone mad. The boulevards are impassable for crowds. I am deaf with the cheers. They cave in! They have been on the verge of it for months. Bluff, it has all been bluff for a long time, and now America has called their hand. They collapse, the Boches. An armistice is arranged. It is certain they restore Alsace-Lorraine. I have cried like a child. Glory to God. France has conquered. Vive la France!"

"Jean safe!" she breathed, smiling.

She seemed to grow younger during the afternoon, before she died.

"And though she knows now it was a lie," said Picq, when they had crossed her hands on her breast, "it is no disappointment to her, since she has him with her now."

VII

A FLAT TO SPARE

At the corner of the rue Baba stands the Maison Séverin, with its board announcing furnished flats to let. One December evening a journalist went to call upon a colleague there. As he climbed the last flight of stairs, a door was opened violently and a gesticulating female appeared. She shrieked defiance over her shoulder, pulled down her sleeves, and descended with such precipitance that she nearly butted Jobic over the banisters.

Dodging her by a miracle, Jobic entered unannounced.

" Your domestic seems to be perturbed, my dear Pariset," he remarked.

" Tiens, you? " said the young widower, panting. " Yes, she has ' returned her apron,' she has resigned the situation, that devil—a situation that offered unsurpassed opportunities for pillage. I am left with the dinner unprepared, and the twins to put to bed—and I ought to be at Batignolles by eight o'clock ! "

" You should marry again," said Jobic.

" I cannot do it in the time. Mon Dieu, just because I mentioned that it was unintelligent of her always to keep the empty wine bottles among the full ones ! It took me a quarter of an hour to get hold of anything to drink. You may tell a bonne that she is an inveterate liar without disturbing her in the least; you may say that she is an habitual thief, and she will accept the truism placidly; but insinuate that she is a fool, and her vanity is in arms at once ! What has brought you here ? ''

" I come to borrow a louis."

" Visionary ! "

" Spendthrift ! What do you do with your salary, then ? The fact is, your rent is an extravagance, and you spend far too much in dressing up your babies; for some time I have had the intention of remonstrating with you on the subject. If you exercised reasonable economy you would be in a position to lend me a louis on your head."

" I am. But the monotonous fatigues me. To attain the charm of variety I propose to lend you nothing at all. I tell you what, however—I can provide you with a job."

" For putting twins to bed my lowest figure is five francs. I will cook the dinner for forty sous, and an invitation to share it."

" The tenders are declined. Listen; you may go to Batignolles and write a column around a communist meeting for me. The kiddies are too young for me to leave them by themselves, and I have been counting on this affair to supply material for my causerie in to-morrow's *Echo*."

" Communist meeting ? " exclaimed Jobic, with distaste; " I do not believe I could borrow any more money under communism than I can now."

" Are we discussing your beliefs? Has your
welfare the remotest interest for me? All I ask
of you is to fill a column. Bring the stuff for me
to sign before you sleep, and I will pay you your
own price for it."

" Cash? "

" Cash."

" It's a deal," said Jobic. " Some sprightly copy
is as good as on your desk. Your editor will not
fail to note a vast improvement in your literary
style."

It was in these circumstances that *L'Echo du
Quartier* contained a column, over Pariset's pen
name of " Valentin Vance," that drove the prettiest
communist in Paris to tears of fury. For not only
did the writer burlesque her impassioned speech,
not only did he poke fun at her theories, and deride
her elocution—he actually made unflattering com-
ments upon her personal appearance.

Not since she embraced the Cause six months
ago had Suzanne Duvivier read anything to
compare with it.

" If I were a married woman," she raged, " my
husband should call the monster out for such
insults ! " And then, since she was an accomplished
pupil at one of the best-known salles for instructing
the fair Parisienne to fence, it occurred to her that
the lack of a husband was no drawback.

Though there were pressing domestic matters to
claim her this morning, she betook herself to
kindred spirits, and burst in upon them to demand
their services.

" Mais, ma chère," gasped mademoiselle Tisserand
and mademoiselle Lagarde, " we have never acted
as seconds in a duel, never ! We implore you to
dismiss the notion; we counsel you to treat the
abuse with the silent scorn that it deserves. The
man might run you through your valiant heart."

" Do we shirk danger, we communists ? " cried
Suzanne.

" Dear comrade, the Cause cannot spare you.
Moreover, every novel with a duel in it that we have
ever read makes it clear that it is the privilege of
the party challenged to choose the weapons. This
monsieur Vance might choose pistols. The novels,
again, indicate that it devolves upon the seconds
to load the pistols, and we have never done such a
thing in our lives. It may also be that you have
never handled one yourself ? "

For a moment Suzanne Duvivier quailed—she
was only twenty-five, and normally no swash-
buckler. If monsieur Vance did choose pistols, she
knew very well she would have to shut her eyes as
she fired. Then the obloquy of the column overwhelmed her anew, and she flung timidity to the
winds.

" We must hope for the best, girls," she said,
resolutely. " If you are my pals you will not
desert me in this hour. I fight for the Cause far
more than for myself. I do not know precisely
what phrases you should employ—consult the
novels !—but the first thing to be done is for you
to present yourselves to the man and desire him
to name the day. You had better not say ' name

the day,' because that has another association, but
he must fix the date. If you can contrive to
suggest that I hanker after pistols, perhaps he will
say ' swords.' Au revoir, my friends. Bear yourselves firmly—look as if you were used to it. Wear
serious hats."

She departed to put in half an hour's practice
at the fencing school, and mademoiselle Lagarde
moaned to mademoiselle Tisserand, " It is terrible,
is it not? However, we need not make frumps of
ourselves, I suppose. I wonder if my toque would
be inappropriate? "

" Not the least in the world," said mademoiselle
Tisserand. " What do you think of my hat with
the bird of paradise? She is right as regards our
demeanour, though—we must be deadly calm.
Let us remember that the dignity of communism
is at stake. The brute must not be allowed to
guess that we are afraid."

A couple of hours later, Pariset, after struggling
with a fire that refused to be lit, and breakfasting
without any coffee, and dressing his twins with some
of their underlinen back in front, gave the concierge
a tip to let him leave them in her loge, and went
forth to the *Echo* building, anathematising his
ex-domestic with continuous fervour on the way.
Arrived there, he found two young women strenuously inquiring for the address of " monsieur
Valentin Vance."

" You behold him, mesdemoiselles," said Pariset.
" What can I have the honour of doing for you? "

The young women looked embarrassed.

" It is you who are the author of this article, monsieur—this infamous calumny ? " queried the plumper of the two.

" Oh ! " exclaimed Pariset, taken aback. " Oh . . . I am speaking to mademoiselle Suzanne Duvivier ? "

" No, monsieur, I am not mademoiselle Duvivier. Neither of us is mademoiselle Duvivier. But we inquire if you are the monsieur Vance who is the author of this article ? "

" Well—er—yes, certainly, I am the author of it."

The pair conferred a moment in undertones. The one in the toque gave the one with the bird of paradise a slight push.

" Then, monsieur, I have the honour to inform you that we are the bearers of a challenge from the lady you have slandered."

" A challenge ? " stammered Pariset. " What do you say ? Is this a joke ? "

" You will find it very far from a joke," put in mademoiselle Lagarde, strategically ; " our principal is a crack shot."

" In that case you may be sure I shall not choose pistols," said Pariset with a smile.

" Ah ! " breathed the girl, dissembling her elation. " You choose swords. No matter."

" No," demurred Pariset. " I do not choose swords, either."

" But—not swords, either ? What, then ? "

" I choose roses. I am a champion with roses, and I have the right to avail myself of my skill."

" Monsieur," cried her companion, peremptorily,
" we shall not be patient with pleasantries ! "

" Nor I with hysteria, mademoiselle. *Comment?*
Do you figure yourself I am going to fight a woman ?
You must be demented."

" You refuse to meet her? "

" Point-blank."

" On the pretext of convention? "

" On the score of manhood."

" Your manhood did not restrain you from
attacking her."

" Was it so bad, the attack? " faltered Pariset,
who had not done much more than glance at Jobic's
masterpiece.

" Pshaw ! " sneered both the girls, as nearly as
their ejaculation can be spelt. " Shame ! How
perfectly disgusting ! You insult a lady, and then
refuse her satisfaction. It is the act of a coward.
Ah ! Oh ! "

" Listen ! " volleyed Pariset. " I will not meet
her if you go on saying ' Ah ! ' and ' Oh ! ' till you
are black in the face. But, to cut it short, she
shall have her satisfaction. I will cross swords with
any man that she appoints as her deputy. All
is said. I await the gentleman's representatives.
Mesdemoiselles, bonjour."

" And now I have got a duel on my hands, as
well as two babies in my arms ! " he reflected.
" Jobic is an imbecile. Why did I trust him?
That sacrée bonne ! her desertion is giving me a
fine time. I should like to wring her neck." He
spent a feverish afternoon at registry offices.

Suzanne was exasperated too. The news of the demand for a deputy was a heavy blow, for she couldn't think of anybody likely to oblige her. Vainly she reviewed the list of her male acquaintances; none seemed to possess all the necessary qualities. Ineligible herself, and unable to find a substitute—what a dilemma! The more provoking because scattered throughout France must breathe several heroic spirits who would have been willing to fight for a nice girl and the guerdon of her gratitude. But she was reluctant to advertise " Duellist wanted," with a portrait of her attractions.

She was removing on the morrow to a furnished flat, and it had been her intention to supervise the removal of some of its dust this morning. Late in the afternoon she ran round to see how matters had progressed without her. A damsel from a registry office in the quarter had undertaken to commence the work punctually at 8 a.m. The flat was in the Maison Séverin. All unconscious that she was to dwell beneath the same roof as the villain she had challenged, Suzanne ascended, sanguine of seeing the clean curtains up.

The damsel hadn't put in an appearance. Either she had received an offer more to her taste, or she had decided to prolong her vacation; there had been no message to explain her caprice.

Suzanne sped to the registry office tumultuously. The *Bureau de Placement des Deux Sexes* was presided over by a very large woman at a very small table. Three of the four employers present were excited ladies, complaining of bonnes who had arranged to take service with them, but who had neither arrived nor written. The fourth was a personable gentleman, awaiting his turn in an attitude of the deepest despondence. Suzanne sat on the bench, by the gentleman's side, while the fat woman strove to appease the three ladies.

" Next, please," she said, eventually. " Monsieur desires ? "

Suzanne heard that monsieur desired a capable bonne à tout faire at once, and that by " at once " he did not mean a fortnight hence, or even the following day—he meant " now."

The proprietress said mechanically that she would see what could be done, and asked for five francs.

" Don't you believe it ! " said the gentleman. " I am a widower and know the ropes—I might part with five francs and remain servantless for a month. Produce a servant. Trot one of your treasures out. Let me get a grip of it and take it away with me, and I will pay you ten—fifteen francs."

" But it happens that there is no servant on the premises this afternoon. Monsieur is not reasonable. He should comprehend that I cannot show him what I have not got."

" It is equally comprehensible, madame, that I cannot pay for what I do not see."

" Next, please," said the fat woman, shrugging her shoulders.

" Madame," began Suzanne, vehemently, " I must ask you to find another femme-de-ménage for me immediately, if you please—your Angélique that I settled with here has never turned up ! "

" There you are ! " cried Pariset.   " Everybody says the same thing."

" Mais, monsieur ! " snorted the proprietress. " Your affair is finished—the business of mademoiselle does not concern you."

" Pardon, madame, my affair is not finished; on the contrary, my need is dire.   I have offspring who clamour for female ministrations, voyons. Mademoiselle will accept my apologies ? "

" They are superfluous, monsieur," said Suzanne, acknowledging his bow.   " But, madame, my case is urgent !   I go into my new appartement in the morning, and there is nobody there yet to shake a mat or light a fire."

" And what a job it is to light a fire ! " put in Pariset, with fellow feeling.

" The life they lead us, these bonnes ! " responded Suzanne.

" Above all, mademoiselle, when one has two little children and is without experience.   Figure yourself my confusion ! "

" Dreadful, monsieur !   I can imagine it."

" What do you expect me to say to you, you two ? " shouted the fat woman, banging the table. " I tell you that there is no bonne waiting just now.   Am I le bon Dieu to create model domestics out of the dust on the office floor ? "

And at this instant the door opened, and there entered briskly a comely wench, wearing an apron, and no hat.

" Ah ! " gasped Pariset and Suzanne together.

" Ah ! " exclaimed the fat woman, jubilant. " Everything arranges itself ! Now I know this one. I recommend her. You can take a place to-day, Marceline ? Good ! It is forty francs a month, as usual, and you sleep in, hein ? "

" Fifty. And I sleep out—with my aunt," said Marceline, promptly, seizing the circumstances.

" I agree," announced the eager clients, in a duet.

" Mais, monsieur——" remonstrated Suzanne, dismayed.

" Mais, mademoiselle——" expostulated Pariset. . . . " Enfin, take her ! I yield her to you. My children pine for her care, but we will suffer ! "

" I am averse from appearing selfish, monsieur——"

" Ah, chivalry forbids that I wrench this unique boon from your arms, mademoiselle."

" No ! She is for monsieur," said Suzanne, in a burst of magnanimity.

The proprietress picked up her pen. " Monsieur resides——? "

" No matter. I renounce my claim in favour of mademoiselle."

The proprietress dipped the pen in the inkpot : " Mademoiselle goes to the Maison Séverin, n'est ce pas ? "

" What ? " cried Pariset. " The Maison Séverin ? It is at the Maison Séverin you have taken a flat, mademoiselle ? Why, that is my address, too ! What storey are you on ? "

" The fourth."

K

" And I ! Listen, an idea, a compromise. If you would be so generous, might you not lend her to me now and then ? "

" But everything arranges itself," repeated the fat woman, joyously. " Mademoiselle and monsieur can share her to perfection. Marceline, you would render service in two little appartements on the same floor ? "

" That is worth more money," said Marceline; and proceeded to estimate the suggestion at a monstrous figure.

However, her views were modified at last. The fat woman made entries in a tattered book. Suzanne heard the gentleman give his name as " monsieur Henri Pariset." Pariset did not hear the lady give her name, because the proprietress, of course, knew it already. Far from suspecting each other's identity, the Challenger and the Challenged exchanged cheerful smiles. Then Marceline was prevailed upon to fetch her box forthwith, and the elated journalist and the charming girl who thirsted for his blood bore their domestic gaily to the rue Baba together.

" How things happen ! " said Pariset, as they went along.

" N'est ce pas ? " said she. " All the same, my flat cannot be got ready by the morning now."

" I don't see why not; my own share of her this evening will be slight. Let her put my babies to bed at once, and then you can have all you want of her. As to my dinner, I will eat at a restaurant."

" Ah, mais non, if it is not your custom ! " said
Suzanne. " She can manage your dinner all right
—she will have no cooking to do for me. I am at
a pension de famille till to-morrow."

And as they reached the house, the concierge
remarked, by way of welcome : " It is not unfortunate that you have returned, monsieur. Your
twins have been disturbing the whole district."

" But they are adorable, your twins ! " exclaimed
Suzanne, with genuine admiration, for now they
were tranquil and beamed. " I cannot pretend to
know whether they are big or small for four years
old, but they are darlings."

" Not bad," said Pariset, who thought the world
of them himself. " Well, then, when Marceline has
tucked them up she shall come to you straightway,
and it is agreed that you are to monopolise her as
long as you like."

Half an hour passed.

" Monsieur ! " cried Marceline, reappearing.

" Eh, bien—you cannot find the children's night-
gowns ? "

" Si, si. The little ones sleep. But the compliments of mademoiselle, and would monsieur be so
amiable as to lend her the feather-brush from his
broom-cupboard ? "

" Take all she wants. How goes it opposite ? "

" There is enough for two persons to do ! "

" I don't doubt it," said Pariset. " Inquire of
mademoiselle whether I can be of any assistance."

But on second thoughts he was prompted to put
the question himself.

In a long blue apron, with her sleeves rolled up, she told him that he couldn't. And he took off his coat and got to work. What a sweeping and a polishing there was ! Nine o'clock had struck when he began to hang the curtains, and the dinner at the pension de famille was a thing of the past.

" Evidently, mademoiselle," he said, from the top of a step-ladder, " you also will have to dine out this evening. What do you say to leaving Marceline to put the finishing touches now, and taking nourishment in my company ? "

" Monsieur," returned Suzanne, " you dizzy me with your neighbourly kindness. If you can turn round without risking your neck, however, you will note that Marceline is absent. She is engaged in improvising a meal for us, and I beg you to accept my invitation."

" Enchanted. Only, as you are still somewhat at sixes and sevens here, may I propose that you invite me to my own flat, instead of yours ? "

So it befell that the bouillon, brought hot in a can from the little greengrocer's across the road, was served at Pariset's table. And Marceline's omelette, created while the cutlets were frizzling on the grille, proved to be delicious.

" Our bonne," remarked the widower, complacently, " might be worse, hein ? "

" I was thinking the same thing," assented Suzanne. " It seems to me that we have done very well for ourselves."

" You smoke a cigarette ? "

" It is one of my consolations."

" I hope that I may be privileged to see you console yourself here often."

" And if you ever have leisure to call upon me for *le feeve o'clock*, monsieur, I shall be charmed. You can hardly excuse yourself on the plea that my address is too remote."

" Believe me," said Pariset, " I warmly felicitate myself on the address; if I may say so, I am daring to foresee a friendship. And it would be very welcome, for I lead a lonely life."

" I, too," she sighed. " I am a painter, I am a communist, but all the same, I am alone."

" Ah, you are a painter, and communist, hein? We shall have subjects to talk about."

" You are surprised? "

" I am, above all, surprised to hear that you are alone. It is difficult to realise how that can be."

" It is true, I assure you. Only to-day I had the strongest need of a man's arm to render me a service, and I could think of no one to ask."

" There are a couple of arms here," announced Pariset, displaying them in an heroic gesture.

" And doughty deeds they have just accomplished for me ! " she laughed.

" No, but seriously——" he urged.

" Oh, seriously, the service that I speak of is far too big for even the best of new friends."

" You are wrong. Without having heard it, I venture to pronounce it just the right size."

" How sincere you are ! And how I appreciate your earnestness ! " she exclaimed. " But it is out of the question."

" I have not yet proved myself worthy of your confidence," he regretted sentimentally. " I understand."

" If you imagine it is *that* "—deep reproach was in her gaze—" I must explain. Have you heard of a journalist called ' Valentin Vance ' ? "

" Yes."

" Well, I sent him a challenge to-day, and he answered that I must find a deputy."

Pariset sat dumfounded. Twice he essayed to articulate, without producing so much as a monosyllable.

At last he stuttered :

" You are mademoiselle Suzanne Duvivier ? I had no idea."

" How stupid of me. You have read his article ? "

" Well—er—I have still not had time to read it very attentively. But I have heard a good deal about it."

" Ah ! Then you do not wonder at my resentment ? " she cried. And, though the twins forbade her to jeopardise his life, she hoped to hear him gallantly offer to fight monsieur Vance.

This was just what Pariset could not do. After his boasted avidity to execute the service, he must wear an air of funking it. His embarrassment was intense ; constraint fell upon them both. Disillusion clouded her eyes. She had begun to like him so much, it grieved her to see him turn tail.

After some very painful seconds he faltered :

" You are disappointed in me ? "

" Disappointed ? "

"Oh, yes. I seem to you a braggart who has backed out of his boast. Yet I assure you I am not to blame. You seek the one service in the world that I am utterly unable to perform."

"Monsieur," replied the girl coldly, "your parental duties are so obviously paramount that it is unnecessary to remind me of them."

"Oh, as to that, one does not expect more than a scratch in a duel, so it is not from parental reasons that I say it can't be done. The reasons are physical. I cannot meet monsieur Vance because . . . I shall sink lower in your esteem with every word . . . I cannot meet him because . . . enfin, Valentin Vance is I !"

"You?" She had started to her feet.

"My pen name."

The silence was awful. She leant on the back of the chair for support. Then, with a dignity that he felt to be superb, she said :

"Monsieur, as a tenant I thank you for your co-operation; as a communist, I ask permission to retire."

"Ah, I implore you to listen ! " raved Pariset.

"It is strange," she added, more spontaneously, "that, since you found me so hideous on the lecture platform, you put yourself out to be so agreeable to me at the registry office."

"I? I find you hideous? " vociferated Pariset. "It was not I who wrote it; not a single word was mine, believe me ! My bonne flounced off last night, and the twins kept me at home. I entrusted the job to a dunderheaded confrère. Ah, mon

Dieu, ' since I found you hideous ' ! The spirituality of your face is an inspiration. I admire you with all my heart. Yes, I shall confess it, with all my heart ! I love you ! Do not condemn me for a column that I did not perpetrate—be merciful, be tender ! I will write others that you shall approve. You shall instruct me—I will gather wisdom from your lips. Yes, at your feet, on our hearth, I will learn from you. I will become a disciple of communism—the mouthpiece of your Cause; I will consecrate my pen to your service. My pen shall annihilate your opponents, though my sword could not chasten monsieur Vance." His arms entreated her. " Suzanne——"

" The appartement of mademoiselle is completely ready ! " proclaimed Marceline. She rushed in, and out again, triumphant.

" It appears to me I shall not need it long," smiled Suzanne, surrendering to his embrace.

VIII

A PORTRAIT OF A COWARD

EVERY Sunday Mrs. Findon went with her two stepdaughters to the cemetery and put flowers on the grave. Every Sunday since her husband's death she had done so—every Sunday for four years, excepting during the month of August, which was passed in the unattractive village where his widowed sister lived. When the melancholy walk was over and they had returned to the house, the Misses Findon used to sit on either side of the fireplace, moist-eyed, and slightly pink about the noses, speaking at long intervals in subdued tones; and their young stepmother would gaze from the window, wondering whether the pretence of mourning a husband she had not loved was to be her lot for life.

When she was twenty her father had said to her, "Belle, Mr. Findon wants to marry you. Don't look like that. He is much older than you are, of course, and it isn't the ideal, but what have you got to look forward to? I'm a pauper, and we both know I can't last much longer, and when I've gone you'll be all alone. How are you to live? You'll be left with about fifty pounds, and waste some of that on crape. It's a ghastly thing for me to lie here and know you'll soon be destitute. He's decent enough in a dull way, and if you were to marry him I should feel I had a right to die."

So she had married him; and Mr. Findon had endeavoured to mould her disposition to his requirements. He moulded so much that it seemed to her he must lament that she wasn't an entirely different person, and she wondered why he had asked her to be his wife. The provincial town to which he took her was depressing, and the furniture and ornaments of his house made her want to shriek, and the people who paid her visits never mentioned any subject that had any interest for her.

More dejecting than the visitors were her step-children. To the two colourless schoolgirls—Amy, fourteen years of age, Mildred nearly sixteen—she had turned eagerly; turned achingly, because no child of her own came to lighten the gloom; and for long she had striven to believe that the slowness of their minds was due to their environment. "They need waking up," she would think, and exhausted herself in efforts to make them fluent. But she found that nothing that was done could make them fluent. And as they grew older, she found that nothing that was said could make them laugh. They laughed only when the wind blew somebody's hat off.

They were sandy, undemonstrative girls, and they had manifested no great affection for their father till he died suddenly five years after the marriage. Then, however, the words " dear father " were for ever on their lips, and a strain of unsuspected sentiment in their nature had opposed itself morbidly to the slightest departure from any domestic arrangement that he had desired. She still remembered Amy's pained stare, and Mildred's startled " I don't think dear father would have liked that ! " when she had diffidently proposed to transfer a huge photograph of his mother from the drawing-room wall to the spare bedroom. She still reproached herself for her compliant " Oh, I won't, then, of course." It was among the first of the concessions that had made the house seem to her a sepulchre. By her stepdaughters' wish, nothing had been altered in his study—not the position of an armchair, or of the footstool. Even to the pipes on the table, and a gum-bottle on the mantelpiece, the room, which was never used now, remained as he had left it last. And every morning for four years she had accompanied Mildred and Amy solemnly to the threshold, and regarded the armchair and the pipes with an air of reverence ; and afterwards sat down to breakfast, thinking that the girls looked as if they had been to the funeral over again. At the beginning, if she had not shrunk from wounding them, she might have hinted that that piece of hypocrisy was horrible to her. Now she could do so no more than she could hint that she did not want to feign bereavement in the cemetery every Sunday, or to take an annual change that was made doleful by the triteness of

Aunt Harriet, and the presence of her invalid son.
At the age of five-and-twenty, the gentleness and
weakness of the woman had committed her to
act a lie. At the age of twenty-nine, the woman
reflected miserably that, unless her stepdaughters
married, she would have to act the lie for life.

The oppressive thought was no new one—and
she had asked stupid people to dinner, and accepted
invitations to wearisome households. She had
urged Mildred and Amy to join the golf and tennis
clubs, though they were apathetic about golf
and tennis, and she usually took them to London
to buy their frocks, instead of to the local High
Street. But girls less becomingly dressed had got
married, and no young man had paid any attentions
to Mildred or Amy. Though Mildred was but
twenty-five, and Amy only twenty-three, both had
already the air of girls destined for spinsterhood.
Sometimes, as she regarded their premature prim-
ness, she found it impossible to suppose that pro-
posals would ever come to them, impossible to
picture either of the staid, angular figures in a man's
arms. Timidly, once, when her dread of a lifetime
spent in Beckenhampton had grown unbearable,
she had nerved herself to suggesting a removal.
" Don't you think we should find it brighter to
live somewhere else ? " she had pleaded. " In
London we should have concerts, and pictures
and things."

" London ? " Amy had faltered, with dismay.
" Oh, no, I shouldn't like that at all."

" Well, it needn't be London, then; but there

are nicer towns than this. What do *you* think, Mildred ? "

" I'm sure we could, none of us, be as happy as we are at home," said Mildred in a shocked voice. " It would seem dreadful to leave the home where dear father used to be with us."

And the little stepmother, her hope extinguished, had found herself murmuring, " Yes, of course, there *is* that, I know." The terms of their father's will had made the house more theirs than hers ; it seemed to her that she lacked the right to persist, even if she could have felt sanguine of persistence prevailing. But what she lacked most of all, of course, was courage. She was good-natured, she was charming, she had some beautiful qualities, but she was without the force of mind to oppose anybody. She was a tender, lovable, and exasperating coward. That is to say, she would have been exasperating if there had been anyone to regret her cowardice, anyone to care much whether she was miserable or not.

And then, one summer, after Mildred had influenza, the doctor recommended Harrogate, instead of the dismal village—and the possibility of Harrogate yielding husbands to the girls quickened the woman's heart. In the season there, among so many men— mightn't there be two to find Mildred and Amy congenial ?

It was she, not they, who pondered so carefully and paid so much for the morning, afternoon, and evening dresses in which they lagged about a fashionable hydro a fortnight later. It was she, not they, who knew a throb of hope when either of them danced twice, monosyllabically, with the same partner, and who welcomed their opportunity to play in an amateur performance, with its attraction of daily rehearsals.

" I don't think we care much for acting," Amy demurred. " I think we would rather look on, like you."

" Dr. Roberts said that Mildred needed to be taken out of herself; if *you* don't go in for it, *she* won't. Oh, I should say yes. It is sure to be a lot of fun, you know."

" I don't think that Mildred and I care much for fun," demurred Amy.

However, the Misses Findon attended the rehearsals—with the dramatic instinct possessed by pasteboard figures on a toy stage. And blankly their stepmother noted that, though young men were ambitious of " polishing their scenes " in alcoves, at various hours, with other girls, no young man's histrionic fervour urged him to any spontaneous polishing with Mildred or Amy.

The thing that did happen at Harrogate was unlooked-for : a man displayed considerable interest in Mrs. Findon herself.

They had spoken first in the hall, where he was sitting when she came out of the breakfast-room with the girls one morning; and on subsequent mornings they had all loitered for ten minutes in the hall; and then, when the rehearsals prevented Mildred and Amy from loitering, she had paused awhile without them. One day, when the rehearsal took place after luncheon, she was surprised to find that she had sat talking to him the whole afternoon. But though their tone had long since grown informal and they talked spontaneously, though he had told her he was in the last fortnight of his leave from India and spoken of his prospects of a judge-ship there, she did not realise how far their acquaint-ance had progressed until he said to her, " You don't look like a happy woman, and yet it doesn't sound to me as if your husband had been all the world to you. If it isn't the loss of your husband that's weighing on you, what's the matter? "

She gazed at him, startled. And still stranger to her than the boldness of his question, was the intimacy of her reply, after she had made it. " Mr. Murray, I'm *not* a happy woman."

From that moment they were not acquaintances —they were friends. Piecemeal he learnt her story, and perceived the weakness of her character. And their confidences were more frequent and prolonged after a hurried letter from Aunt Harriet, saying that " her dear boy had passed away, and that it would help her to bear her cross if dear Mildred and Amy would go to her for two or three days." A week slid by, and they were with her still. And meanwhile Mr. Murray and Mrs. Findon fell in love with each other.

It was her first breath of romance. A father's ailments, encompassing her girlhood, had excluded sentimental episodes. To marriage she had been moved by nothing but docility. She would soon be thirty—and for the first time she found a strange

pulsating promise in the birds' twittering when she
woke; lingered at a looking-glass, and turned
back to it, that a man might approve. She eyed
intently time's touches on her face, noting with
new sensitiveness that it showed her age. She
knew, for the first time, restlessness if one man
was absent; and if he was present, knew impatience
of all others who were present too. And she
sparkled at her own blitheness; and but for the
recurring thought that it would all be over soon,
she lived in Eden for a week.

They had been speaking of her stepdaughters,
and he had said, " The first time I saw you with
them I wondered what the relationship was. You
can't have much in common with them? You
must have hoped to see them marry, haven't you? "

" Do you think they will? " she asked.

" Oh, I don't know. It doesn't follow, because
one finds no charm in a girl oneself, that nobody
else will find any. I've known men crazy about
women that I wouldn't have turned my head to
look at—and men that were by no means fools.
Isn't there anybody in Beckenhampton? "

" There aren't many chances for a girl in Beckenhampton. Besides, they don't care for young men's
society—that's one of the reasons why men don't
find much to say to them, I think. I hoped something might come of their staying here, but——"

" But a man has wanted to talk to *you*, instead."

Could she control her voice? " Oh, that's a
different thing."

" Why is it a different thing ? "

" I meant that I hoped it might lead to something for them—I wasn't thinking of friendship."

" *I'm* not thinking of friendship; your friendship wouldn't be much use to me out there. I want you to be my wife. Will you ? "

They were in the garden, after dinner. From the ladies' orchestra in the hall came the barcarolle from *The Tales of Hoffmann.* In sentiment she was in her teens.

" I can't," she said, in a whisper.

" I'm so fond of you. Do you know I've never heard your name ? "

She told him her name.

" Belle, I'd be so good to you. Don't you like me ? "

She turned to him. No one could see them. The first kiss of her first love—moonlight, and the barcarolle. Though she did not recognise it, there was a single instant in which she was capable of any weakness. But she was not capable of strength.

" I can't," she repeated. " How can I ? To marry again ! I couldn't say such a thing to them. What would they—I couldn't do it."

" I don't understand. You ' can't marry me ' because they wouldn't like it ? You don't mean that ? Or is it because you don't think you ought to leave them ? "

" Both."

" But—good heavens ! . . . Besides, there's this aunt they've gone to—they could live with her. You aren't telling me—you can't mean you won't

L

marry me because you imagine it's your duty to
sacrifice our happiness for the sake of two young
women you don't care about? You know you
don't care about them! It's mad! I need you
more than they do; I can make you happier than
they do. I shall never be a millionaire, but I
shall come into a bit by and by, and I can make
things bright for you at home, one day. You'd
have rather a good time out there, for that matter.
I *want* to make things bright for you—I want to see
you what you were meant to be. You've never
had your youth yet, you've been done out of it;
I want to give it to you, I want you to forget what
it means to feel depressed. That'd be just my
loveliest joy, to see you in high spirits, laughing,
waking up younger instead of older, growing more
like a girl every day. . . . People'd begin to take
me for your father! That'd be rough on me,
wouldn't it?"

She looked, misty-eyed and smiling, at this
man who had transfigured life for her.

" I know it sounds silly of me."

" That's meek," he laughed. " Very well, then.
As soon as they come back we'll tell them. Perhaps
they won't mind as much as you think—they
aren't so devoted to you, are they?"

" It isn't that. Their father's memory means
so much to them—they'll think it so awful of me.
And——"

" And what?"

" You don't know everything—I haven't told
you all about it. It sounds hideous, I know, but

I couldn't help it—I drifted into it. I—I've had to pretend so much. Pretend to miss him, I mean. All the time. Every day. I—— To tell them that it wasn't true—— How can I?"

"You wouldn't be the only woman who had loved twice; other women have cared for their husbands, and married again."

"It has been all the time," she muttered, shame-faced. "Even since we have been here I've had to—— Just before they went, we sent flowers to the cemetery and I was supposed to—I mean, I had to pretend to be sorry we couldn't take them ourselves. What a hypocrite I shall seem! What'll they say?"

He grasped her hands, and held her tight, and told her what *he* would be willing to do for *her*— and though he was older than she, and looked it, he talked like a boy. "Do you disbelieve me?" he asked. "And if you don't disbelieve me, won't *you* face a little awkwardness for *me*? If it comes to that, *I* can speak to them first. Once the news is broken, the worst'll be over for you. What a baby you are, darling! May I call you a baby the moment I'm engaged to you, Mrs. Findon, madam? Oh, you little timid, foolish, sweetest soul, fancy talking about missing all our happiness for life, to avoid a bad half-hour! It'd be a funny choice, wouldn't it, Belle my Belle?"

She nodded, radiant; and aglow with the courage he had communicated, she thought she could have proclaimed her intention straightway, if the young women had returned then.

They did not, however, return at all. Next morning the post brought from them the news that they felt too sad to find Harrogate congenial now, and that they would rather be at home. They were going back to Beckenhampton the " day after to-morrow."

It meant that her precious hours here were numbered. She showed the letter disconsolately to Murray.

" I shall have to go this afternoon," she said.

" I don't see what for—I don't see why you should be dragged away at a minute's notice. You're not a child to be ' sent for.' "

" Oh, I must go," she sighed; " I *must* get there before them, to see to things."

They stood together in the hall—the hall that he knew would look so pathetically blank to him this afternoon.

" We haven't had long, have we ? " he said. " How I'm going to hate everybody in this hydro when you've gone !—the people that mention you, and the people that don't mention you; every single one of them; because I shall be missing you in every second and they'll all be chattering and scandalmongering just the same. When shall I hear from you ? You'll tell them as soon as you see them—you won't put it off, even for an hour ? Oh, my darling, don't think I'm not alive to all that's beautiful in you, but "—he tried to smile— " you *are* a little bit of a coward where they're concerned, aren't you ? Keep remembering you're free to do as you like. If they aren't pleased, they can be displeased. You haven't got to ask their permission. It's a perfectly simple statement— you're 'going to marry me.' They haven't a shadow of right to complain. If you'll remind yourself of that, it'll make it smoother for you. . . . I wish we could have had a day together first—away from all this crew, I mean. Couldn't you make it to-morrow instead? We'd have a car and go some-where. Couldn't you, Belle?"

" I can't," she said wistfully. " It'd be heavenly. But I can't. I ought to go upstairs and pack now."

" All right, little woman," said he; " I don't want to make it worse for you. Go along, then. I may see you off, mayn't I? And I'll 'phone at once about your passage on the boat. And I'll come to Beckenhampton the instant you send for me. And we're to be married by special licence next week. Oh, isn't it great! And then your new life begins—the laughter life, the girl life. I'm going to wipe out that troubled look they've put in your eyes—I'm going to make you self-willed, make you tyrannise over me."

" Tyrannise over the Judge! Wouldn't it be a shame?" she laughed. " What a reward for you!"

" I don't know," he said; " I believe I'd like it—it's time you did a little tyrannising. I can't kiss you, darling, because somebody's coming down the stairs, but look at me and let's pretend!"

Downcast as she felt, as the train bore her from him, she felt firm. She could not view the

ordeal before her as lightly as he—he did not understand, she told herself; it was natural that he
shouldn't—but she was resolved to meet it without
delay, and to be bold in the face of the consternation
she foresaw. How easy it would have been but
for the insincerities she had been guilty of, the
craven insincerities ! It was her own horrible
hypocrisy, not her stepdaughters' disapproval,
that made the task so difficult. As she dwelt
upon the difficulties, as she realised the almost
incredible shock she was about to deal, the fortitude within her faded, and during the latter half
of the journey it was with thankfulness she reflected
that she would not have to confront the situation
that day.

It should be directly they arrived, though !
She vowed it.

She had watched tremulously till nearly three
o'clock, when a cab rumbled to the house at last;
and her heart turned sicker still as she saw that
her stepdaughters were accompanied by their aunt.

" We persuaded her to come."

" I'm afraid I shall be a sad visitor for you, my
dear."

" They were quite right. The change will do
you good."

They explained that they had lunched early,
and they sat awhile in the drawing-room, with their
hats and coats on—her sister-in-law oppressive
with much crape; the young women also wearing
black dresses, very badly made.

" A glass of wine, Harriet? You must be tired after the journey." She rang the bell.

Sipping the port, and alternately nibbling a biscuit, and flicking crumbs from her lap, Aunt Harriet was taciturn and tearful. And she had little to say between tea and dinner, excepting when she spoke huskily of her son's last hours. But in the evening her thoughts reverted to the " happy days she had spent in the house when her dear brother was alive," and she discoursed on them, remarking how " sadly different it seemed now."

" It was a terrible loss for you, Belle," she moaned. " But the parting is only for this life. That's all, my dear, only for this life. You'll meet again where there are no partings. You must keep thinking of that. It's only faith that helps us all to bear up."

And the hypocrite, loathing her hypocrisy, heard herself answer, " Oh, I know! Oh yes ! "

At Harrogate the orchestra would be playing now, and he was wondering if she had told them yet ! She gazed before her helplessly. She would have to put it off till to-morrow.

Said Mildred, " I daresay Aunt would like to go to bed early."

" If you'll all excuse me, dear, I think I should."

" I think we're all of us ready, aren't we? " murmured Mrs. Findon.

And as they got up and filed from the room, Amy said in sacerdotal tones, " There's one thing

we want to do, isn't there, before we go upstairs
to-night?" And, like one who performs a rite,
she opened the study door; and on the threshold
they drooped devoutly.

"O God, forgive me, and help me to be truthful!"
prayed the hypocrite when she was alone.

The morrow was Sunday, and in the morning
they went to church; and after service they walked
dismally to the cemetery. At dinner she could
scarcely swallow. She felt faint, and her hands
trembled when the return to the drawing-room
was made. It had to be now! Her sister-in-law
was settling herself for a nap. Amy turned listlessly
the pages of a book. Mildred, her shallow eyes
upturned, and her head slightly sideways, wore an
air of pious resignation to some unexpressed
calamity. Turning from the window, with a gulp,
the coward stammered :

"Oh . . . after you had gone from Harrogate,
Mr. Murray asked me to marry him."

The silence seemed to her to last for minutes.

"To do *what?*" gasped Amy.

"*Well!*" exclaimed Mildred. "It didn't take
long to put *him* in his place, I hope. What
impudence!"

"He had an impudent look," said Amy.

"Some man who was staying at the hydro where
you were?" inquired Aunt Harriet. "Fancy!
That's the worst of those large places. But I
shouldn't let it worry you, my dear. It isn't
worth worrying about. Very likely he didn't mean
any harm by it. He didn't understand, that's

all—didn't know your heart was buried with him
who's gone."

"Disgusting, *I* call it," said Mildred. "But
Aunt's quite right—we needn't talk about it. . . .
I thought this morning—I don't know if you noticed
it—that the saxifrage on the grave had gone rather
thin; there was a gap here and there. I think
we'd better see the superintendent. It isn't what
it ought to be, by any means."

She stood struggling to say the rest—she
struggled with all the puny will that was within
her. And so unfit was she to struggle, that on
surrendering, her paramount emotion was relief.
She said, " Yes, we'll see him about it, and have
some more."

She had intended to write to Murray in time
for the evening collection. But she could not
write that she had kept her word, and she shrank
from writing that she had paltered with it. She
lay sleepless, crying with mortification. Once a
desperate impulse to be done with her compliance
then and there, pulled her up, and she thrust on her
dressing-gown; but her mind quailed even as she
reached the door, and she sank on to the edge of
the bed, procrastinating—and then crept back
between the sheets.

She could not write that she had kept her word
on the next day either, nor during the two days
that followed. The just thing to them both would
have been to write him exactly what had happened,
but as she was a woman, the thing natural to her
when she was to blame was to behave worse still

by not writing at all. A feeble attempt she made, but . . . what was there to say, excepting that she had failed? In every moment she was conscious of his waiting; she realised the glances that he cast at that letter-rack over the console table, and saw his mouth tighten at every disappointment that it dealt. And she was fond of him. Yet it was beyond her to sustain the effort to confess herself demeaned.

He telegraphed : " Coming to you by the seven o'clock train to-morrow Friday morning."

From her bedroom window, before breakfast, she saw the boy crossing the road with the message, and she darted downstairs and took it from him before the double knock could crash. No one was aware, when the family group made their matins to the study, that in her pocket she had a telegram from a lover. No one surmised, when she served the eggs and bacon, that she was questioning, terrified, how to keep his coming secret. If any of them were in, when the maid said that he was asking for her? She would be tongue-tied. And they—how insulting they'd be to him ! It would be awful . . . awful, unless she were to prepare them, unless she were to say now that she had heard from him and that they must receive him properly. She knew she wasn't going to say it, but she imagined the sensation if she said it : " Mr. Murray's calling this morning. You've made a mistake—I accepted him." She shivered at the mere notion, at fancying how horror would distort their faces.

Just after she had been shamming in that room !
. . . She would make an excuse to go out—she'd
meet him at the station.

It was going to be very painful—she wished
he weren't coming. In love with him though she
was, she knew that she wished he weren't coming.
And in that moment it was borne upon her that
her expectation of marrying him had died days
ago. She could never go through with it ! She
would have to tell him so—and he wouldn't understand, wouldn't make allowances for her. He
had not understood at Harrogate. He'd reproach
her, tell her she had treated him badly. And she'd
have to sit there, in the waiting-room, trying not to
cry, with people looking on. . . .

If she could have been picked up in his arms
and carried off this morning, without coming back
to the house at all ! That would be nice. The
girls and Harriet might say what they chose,
if she hadn't got to listen to it. But he wouldn't
ask her to go like that; she would have to propose
it herself. How could she ? Besides, when she
went out to meet him she couldn't even take a
suit-case. . . . Oh, what good would it do to meet
him ? Pain for nothing. He thought he would
be able to argue her into it, make her promise
over again. Wretched. And very likely she *would*
promise—and then what was she going to do ?
She would feel worse then than she felt now. It
would have been far better for them not to see each
other. If she told the servant—— She couldn't
say " Not at home," that would sound dreadful.

He might be here soon, she supposed, unless he had to wait long for the change of trains. If she did mean to go to the station, she ought to go directly she had given orders to the cook. Walking into misery with her eyes open ! And walking back with her heart in her shoes. It wouldn't be any easier to say it to them later than it was at this minute—and she would know it even while he was wringing the promise from her. Oh, what was he coming for, to make things worse still? He might have known by her not having written to him—— She pushed back her chair with vexation.

After breakfast, when the beds were being made, Mrs. Findon said :

" Doreen, if anybody calls this morning—a gentleman—say we're away from home for a few days. You understand? For a few days—all of us. Oh, and, Doreen, if he asks where we are, you don't know."

More than six years have gone by since Mrs. Findon peeped, breathless, as Mr. Murray got into a cab again and was driven out of her life. And now when she reads in her newspaper, every day, on one page or another, how sublimely mankind has progressed by relapsing into barbarism, and that the new human nature is purged of frailties that were inherent in men and women until the 4th August 1914, she vaguely wonders how it is that her household, and her social circle, and Beckenhampton at large, and she herself have not had their characters regenerated, like the rest of the world. For each morning she goes with the Misses Findon to gaze upon the study, and each Sunday she goes with them to gaze upon the grave; and on their return, while the Misses Findon sit by the fireplace, speaking at long intervals, in subdued tones, their stepmother stares from the window, knowing that her pretence of mourning a husband she did not love will continue as long as she lives. And when she looks back on her romance, she marvels—not at the recreancy of her submission, but that once she briefly dared to dream she would rebel.

IX

THE BOOM

At this time of day I do not mind publishing the facts. It happened a few weeks after those pillars of the State—Thibaudin and Hazard—disappeared from Paris with a couple of million francs. They were leading the police a pretty dance, and people said, " Ah, they are probably at the world's end by this time ! " I used to think to myself how securely a man who had a mind to do so might lie hidden within an hour's journey of the Grand Boulevard. It was really the disappearance of Thibaudin and Hazard that originated my Idea.

I was manager at that period of the Théâtre Suprême, where we were very soon to produce Beauregard's play, *Omphale*. I descried a way to attract additional attention to our project. I went to see Beauregard one October morning, and gave him a shock. He was breakfasting in bed.

" Bonjour, maître," I said. " Are you too much occupied to talk business ? "

" Panage," exclaimed the dramatist, " if you have come to demand any more mutilations of the manuscript, I tell you without parleying that no consideration on earth will induce me to yield. There is a limit; mon Dieu, there is a limit! Rather than cut another line, or substitute another syllable I will put the contract in the fire."

"Dear friend, you have evidently slept ill and are testy this morning," I said. "Compose yourself. I come to exhilarate you with a great scheme."

He still eyed me apprehensively, and to pacify him I made haste to explain, "It has nothing to do with any alterations in the play."

"Ah!" He breathed relief, and dipped his croissant in his cup.

"It is a scheme for booming it."

My host was forthwith genial. A smile suffused his munching face, and he offered me a cigarette.

"I ask your pardon if I was abrupt," he said. "As you surmise, I passed a bad night. A boom? Well, you know my views on the subject of booming. The ordinary puff preliminary is played out. One needs something novel, Panage, something scholarly. 'Scholarly' is the word. For *Omphale*, a play of pre-Hellenic times, one needs the boom scholarly, classical, and grandiose."

"You voice my own sentiments," said I. "One needs nothing less than a production of 'unrivalled accuracy' — costumes 'copied from designs discovered in Crete and dating back to the dim days of the Minotaur.' That would look tasteful in print, would it not? Alors, what do you say to our going to Crete and discovering them?"

"Crete?" stammered Beauregard. Have I

mentioned that he was fat and indolent and had never travelled further than Trouville?

" What think you of exploring the Minotaur's lair? " I questioned. " Of penetrating to the apartments of Phædra? Of examining with your own eyes the labyrinth of Ariadne? "

" I? " he ejaculated.

" You and I together, my old one! Our adventures would make pretty reading, hein? Would not all Paris be chattering about your *Omphale*? What a fever of impatience for the first night! Think of the effect such paragraphs would have on the advance booking."

The corpulent Beauregard lay back on the pillows, pale and mute. I had spoken too earnestly for him to suspect that I was pulling his leg, and I could see that he was very seriously perturbed. His mind was torn in halves between his longing for the advertisement and his horror of the exertion and expense. After a moment he sat up, perspiring, and wrung my hand.

" Panage," he cried, " you are a man of genius! Your idea is most brilliant; I have never heard its equal. With all my heart I congratulate you. I, alas! cannot accompany you on account of my wife's ill-health, but *you* are free. Go, mon ami! Your inspiration will crowd your theatre."

His wife's health was offensively robust. I shook with laughter so unrestrained that the cigarette fell out of my mouth.

" Let me be a trifle more explicit," I said. " It is not essential to my scheme that either you or I should actually go to Crete. It is only essential that we should be reported to have gone there. I propose that we should blazon our departure in all the journals—we might give them interviews in the midst of our packing—and that we should then retire for two or three months to some secluded spot near at hand where there will be nobody to recognise us. I shall confide only in Verdeille, my secretary; I can rely on him, and he will keep the Press well supplied with anecdotes of our vicissitudes during our absence. Mon Dieu! We will make Paris bubble and boil with anticipation."

He was admiring, but timid. "Don't you think it would be very risky?" he demurred. "If our imposture were found out? It would be ruin. For example, what spot?"

"Well, I am not prepared with spots at the instant; I came to you on the effervescence of the notion. But somewhere off the beaten track. One can hide very effectually without going far— I would not mind wagering that Thibaudin and Hazard are lying low in some hamlet. While the police are watching Marseilles and Havre, or picturing them already in South America, they are probably concealed within an easy run of the gare St. Lazare, waiting till the search is relaxed. What about one of the little seaside places in Normandy—have you ever stumbled on one of them a day after the season finished? There is nobody left but the garde-champêtre."

He shivered. "Three months of it?" he queried piteously.

M

" Our investigations, which we undertake ' to complete the previous labours of the archæologists,' ought to be thorough," I pointed out. " Is it not worth our while to suffer a little tedium for such an end ? Lift your gaze to the cash that will accrue, Beauregard. Dwell upon the box-office besieged. Positively we shall double the value of your play. Also you can take plenty of exercise and improve your figure."

" I abhor exercise," he murmured.

" And you could keep early hours and prolong your life."

" My life is a series of vexations—to prolong it would be fatuous."

" Further, everybody will say what a conscientious artist you are; I don't mind asserting that your passion for accuracy is sweeping me to the Minotaur's lair against my will."

" Well, I will think about it," he said heavily.

He promised to write to me on the morrow.

There was no difficulty about finding a summer resort forsaken enough in October—the difficulty was to find one sufficiently animated to boast an hotel that remained open; and at last I authorised Verdeille to provide us with a furnished châlet. Of these he had reported an unlimited choice everywhere. The resort finally approved for our purpose contained thirty furnished châlets, and they were all to be let with alacrity until the following July. We took ours until February. I had extracted Beauregard's consent, and a fortnight later I hustled him into a cab. He looked as if he were being removed for a kill-or-cure operation, and I am sure he had half a mind to break his word even when we were in the train. On the journey I perused with pleasure *Le Matin*, and the current issue of *L'Illustration*, in which the programme of our imaginary trip was set forth with a wealth of invention that did me credit. The deception, in fact, had been engineered so eloquently that at moments I had almost begun to fancy we were really bound for Crete.

We travelled to Dieppe, and then a cab crawled into a void with us—the motor service, we learnt, was discontinued for the next nine months. The châlet was a high, gaunt house called " Les Myosotis." A peasant, who represented the agence de location, stood at her door to wonder at our arrival. A primitive bonne, whom Verdeille had engaged to attend upon us, appeared to entertain doubts of our sanity. We entered the scene as messieurs " Poupard," and " Bachelet." It was *my* precaution to choose names beginning with a P and a B ; I thought of the initials on our luggage, and our washing—the dramatist had overlooked that point.

Well, I shall not pretend that I was in for a rollicking time. I have a high esteem for Beauregard in the theatre, but Beauregard in a village was unspeakable. His lamentations linger with me yet. We had nothing to do, except to walk in the mud and regard the shutters of the twenty-nine other châlets. At seven o'clock in the evening, the distant lighthouse, and the lamp in our own salon afforded the only lights discoverable for miles round.   That fat Parisian's melancholy, his reproaches, his attitudes of despair, defy description.   Even when the weather improved, he would perceive no virtue in it.   I exclaimed once, " What a beautiful sky to-night ! "   He replied, " It *would* be beautiful from the Place de la Concorde ! " He had brought a cartload of novels—and before we had been in the place a week he was complaining that he had nothing to read.

" I shall die if I remain any longer," he declared. " I shall be buried here, I foresee it.   The climate doesn't agree with me.   Honestly, I feel very unwell.   I ought to return to Paris, it is my duty —I have my wife to consider."

" You were never so well in your life," I remonstrated sharply.   " Rubbish ! there's no escape now, you've got to see it through.   Foretaste the triumph of *Omphale* and be blithe."

" How much will a triumph be worth to me if I am dead ? " he wailed.   " Mon Dieu ! what an existence, what demoniac desolation !   I shudder when I wake in the morning; the thought of the terrible day before me weighs me down.   I have scarcely the energy to put on my socks.   To wash my neck exhausts me.   Is there nothing, nothing to be done for an hour's respite—is there no entertainment within reasonable distance ? "

" My beloved ' Bachelet,' " I said, " you forget; at a place of entertainment we might be recognised. Besides, there isn't any."

He threw up his arms.   " It is like being in gaol,

word of honour! Who directed you to this fatal
hole, where a postman collects letters only when he
pleases—this desert, where Monday's *Matin* drifts
by Tuesday night? By what perverse ingenuity
did you contrive to find it? How long have we
endured it now?"

"Ten days," I told him cheerfully. "Why, we
have only got about eighty more!"

He groaned. "It seems like centuries. My
misgiving, of course, is that it will drive me to
intemperance: such ordeals as this develop the
vice. The natives themselves are staggered by
our presence; they whisper about me as I pass.
Children follow me up the roads, marvelling; if the
population sufficed, I should be followed by crowds.
I tell you, we are objects of suspicion; we are a
local mystery; they conclude we must have ' done
something.' Also the laundress here is a violent
savage—she is not a laundress at all. I had six
new collars when we came, six collars absolutely
new from the box—and this devil has frayed them
already. I would never have believed it could be
accomplished in the time, but she has managed it.
Six collars absolutely new from the box!"

Don't imagine that he had finished! don't
suppose that it was merely a bad mood. It was
the kind of thing I had to bear from him daily,
hourly—from the early coffee to the latest cigarette.

One afternoon, when I had gone for a stroll
without him, a contretemps occurred. I had
entered the outfitter's, and stationer's, and tobac-
conist's and provision merchant's—the miniature

shop was the only one in the place that had not
closed until the following summer—to obtain a
pair of shoelaces. That the clod-hoppers cackled
about our sojourn was a small matter to me, and
I paid no more heed to the woman's curious stare
to-day than usual. But I was to meet another
stare !

As I waited for my change, a shabby young man
came in to ask for a copy of *Le Petit Journal*, and
a toy for five sous. *Le Petit Journal*, which I had
just read, contained the latest details of my explora-
tions in Crete, and instinctively I looked round.
His eyes widened. I did not know him from Adam ;
but it was evident that *he* knew *me*, at least by
sight ! I turned hot and cold with confusion.

Grabbing at my coppers, I hurried out, wondering what I had better do if he addressed me.
Before I had time to solve the question I heard
him striding at my heels. With a deprecating bow
that told me he had favours to solicit, he exclaimed,
" Monsieur Panage ! "

" You are mistaken," I said promptly.

" Oh, monsieur, I beg you to hear me," he cried,
" I entreat you ! In the theatre you are for ever
inaccessible—will you not spare an instant to me
here ? "

He was so sure of my identity that I realised it
would be indiscreet of me to deny it any longer.
Since I could not deceive, my only course was to
ingratiate him.

" What do you want ? " I asked, fuming.

" Monsieur," he broke out, " I am an actor. I

have been acting in the provinces since I was a
boy. I have played every kind of part from farce
to tragedy. I have talent, but I have no influence,
and the stage doors of Paris are shut and barred
against me ! No manager will listen to me, because
I am too obscure to obtain an introduction to him;
no one will believe that I have ability, because I
cannot get a chance to prove it. Oh, I know very
well what a liberty I have taken in speaking to you,
but I want to get on, I want to get on—I implore
you to give me a trial ! "

He had me in a nice fix. Apparently he was
unaware that I was believed to be in Crete, but he
would soon learn it by the newspaper in his pocket,
and if I snubbed him he would certainly give me
away. He could hold me up to ridicule—I should
be the laughing-stock of Paris. It was a fine
situation for me. I, the director of the Théâtre
Suprême, was compelled to temporise with this
provincial mummer !

I scrutinised him in encouraging silence, as if
mentally casting him for a part. I saw hope
bounding in him.

" Ah ! " I said thoughtfully. " Y-e-s. . . . What
is your favourite line ? "

" Character, monsieur," he panted. " And, of
course, I would accept a very small salary, a very
small salary indeed."

I did not doubt it. I could picture him strutting
and ranting on the boards of a booth for a louis
a week, and holding himself lucky when he earned
that.

" Walk on a little way with me," I said graciously; " we can talk as we go along. I should
have to see you do something before I could consider
you, you know; I must be sure that you are capable.
Even the gentleman who plays the servant at the
Suprême and hasn't a single word to utter is an
experienced comedian. You are not playing any-
where in the neighbourhood? you are not in a
travelling theatre about here? "

" No, monsieur," he sighed, " I am out of an
engagement; I am here because this is where I
live."

" Rather remote from the dramatic world? "
I suggested, smiling; " something of a drawback, is
it not? " His simplicity in crediting me with the
notion of recruiting the Suprême from a travelling
theatre tickled me nearly to death.

" A grave drawback, monsieur," he agreed.
" But I am not alone—I have a child, and she is
too delicate to thrive in a city."

" A good many delicate children have thriven in
Paris," I remarked.

" In thriving households, monsieur—in healthy
quarters. Paris is dear, and I am poor—*my* child
would be condemned to a slum. I should see her
fade away. Better to be a barnstormer all my life
than lose my child. She is all I have left to love."

" There is your art," I said, humbugging him.

" My art? " He gave an hysterical laugh. A
nervous, jumpy fellow, without a particle of repose.
" Listen, monsieur, listen. I am an actor, and
if I could demolish the barrier that keeps me out,

I might be a great one; but I confess to you that I would abandon art and cast figures on an office stool, or break flints on a road, and thank God for the exchange, if it would buy my child a home! I want money. I want to give my child the comforts that other children have. That's *my* ambition. I have no loftier pose than fatherhood. My prayer is, not applause, and compliments, and notoriety, not the petty pleasure of hearing I have equalled one favourite or eclipsed another; my prayer is—to give things to my child! I want to buy her nourishing food, and a physician's advice, and the education of a gentlewoman. I want the money to send her to the South when it snows, and to the mountains when it's hot. I want to see her laughing in a garden, like the rich men's children in Paris that you spoke of. I stand and watch them sometimes—when I go there to beg at stage doors till an understrapper kicks me out."

" Well, well, the sort of things you desire are not so expensive," I said suavely. " Some day your salary may provide them all."

" You think it possible, monsieur? Really? " His haggard eyes devoured me.

" You have only to make one success. After that, you will be grossly overpaid, like every other star."

" If I could but do it ! " he gasped. " If I could only convince a Paris manager that I have it in me! Year after year I've hoped, and tried, and failed to get a hearing. You may judge my desperation by my audacity in stopping you in the streets.

change of intentions would have spared us much. His dilatoriness exposed us to a thunderbolt. We had pealed the bell in his bedroom for the lamp, and when the door was opened at last, I turned to utter a sharp complaint of the delay. To my surprise, I saw that a stranger was walking in. There was a fraction of a second in which I stared indignantly, waiting for an apology for his blunder. Then it was as if my heart slipped slowly to my stomach, and I felt catastrophe in the air, even before I heard his rustic, official tones. He arrested us as Thibaudin and Hazard!

Behind me I heard Beauregard's dressing-case drop with a thud.

Our eyes met, and we stood petrified, realising the impossibility of concealing our names. In my terror of the public scandal that was imminent, my clothes stuck to my skin. Curs, as well as criminals, we looked. I rather fancied that our provincial captor was relieved to see what knock-kneed miscreants he had to deal with.

" You bungling idiot ! " I gasped. " I am monsieur Panage, of the Théâtre Suprême; this gentleman is monsieur Beauregard, of the Académie Française. You shall suffer for this outrage ! "

He shifted his feet slightly. It was the least bit in the world, but that motiveless movement betrayed misgiving; I deduced from it that, in his eagerness to distinguish himself, he had taken more responsibility upon his bucolic shoulders than sat quite comfortably on them. I flung my card to him. " Look ! "

" What of it ? " he said surlily. " What evidence
is this? I see you were preparing for flight. No
violence ! "—Beauregard had impotently wrung
his hands—" I have men in the passage. You will
offer your explanations in the proper quarter.
Come ! " He advanced upon me.

" Now, listen to me," I cried, backing in a panic.
" Put so much as a finger on us and you are ruined.
Not only will I have you discharged from the
Force, I will have you hounded out of any employ-
ment that you find to the end of your days. It is
I who say it ! You have no excuse : we bear no
resemblance whatever to Thibaudin and Hazard.
If you were of Paris you would know as much ! "

Again he faltered. Again he saw distinction
within his grasp. The workings of a dull intelligence, a fool's passion for promotion, supplied a
fascinating study, even in my fear. " Hollow
cheeks, small grey moustache, slight stoop ? " he
recited, eyeing me. His sheep's gaze travelled to
Beauregard. " Age forty, bald at crown. Fat."

" Is he the only fat man in France, fool? We
can call all Paris to prove who we are ! "

" Monsieur will have his opportunity to prove it
elsewhere," he returned stubbornly. But the
" monsieur " hinted that I was impressing him
against his will.

Beauregard began to collect his wits. " If we
are compelled to prove it elsewhere, it will be the
end of *you !* " he raged. " Better be convinced
in time, I warn you. Hazard *is* fat, yes; *I* am,
perhaps, a little plump."

us spoke any more.   The lamp having still made no appearance, I lit the candles.   I do not forget that long half-hour in Les Myosotis.   The yokel himself grew restless at last—he rose and went into the corridor again.

"Hark," exclaimed Beauregard suddenly, "the man has come back.   Can you hear Manesse? Listen."

"I cannot distinguish," I murmured, straining my ears to the door.

Some minutes passed.   To our dismay, our oppressor re-entered alone.   Perplexity darkened his brow.   He hesitated before he broke the suspensive hush.

"Monsieur Manesse agrees that this afternoon he met monsieur Panage," he announced.   "*But*" —he raised a forensic forefinger—"that does not establish that either of *you* is monsieur Panage. Monsieur Manesse is occupied in telling a fairy tale to his little daughter and cannot spare the time to come here to identify you.   Enfin, you will accompany me to the commissaire de police, and you will obtain the evidence in due course."

"Sacré tonnerre!" I screamed.   It was the last straw.   That strolling player declined to "spare the time," that mountebank neglected Me!

I saw crimson.   I paced the room, raving. "What did he say?" I spluttered.   "What were the ruffian's words?"

"My man reports that the gentleman replied, 'Monsieur Panage must have had immense diffi- culty in recollecting my name.   He would not stir

an inch to save my life—why should *I* take a walk
for *him?* ' "

I sat down. I felt dizzy. I feared I was going
to be extremely ill. The man himself seemed
moved by my collapse—or increasingly uncertain
of his position. He said, " Perhaps a note might
be effectual? Alors, if monsieur wishes to write,
I will wait."

" Give me your fountain-pen, Beauregard.

" But "—again the forefinger was uplifted—
" there must be no secret instructions. I must
be satisfied there is no private meaning in the
note."

" Good heavens ! What am I permitted to say ? "

He pondered. " ' To monsieur Paul Manesse :
Monsieur——' Has monsieur written 'Monsieur' ? "

" Yes, yes; go on ! "

" ' I am now convinced that you can act. I
hereby engage you, at the trifling salary of two
hundred and fifty francs a week, for prominent
parts in my next three productions at the Théâtre
Suprême.' "

The silence was sensational.

" Who the devil are you? " I stuttered, when I
found my voice.

" Paul Manesse, monsieur," he told me—" your
new comedian, if you sign."

I signed. You have heard how we boomed
Omphale and I found a star ! That jolly little
Manesse girl has a rich papa to-day.

N

X

PILAR NARANJO

In one of the dullest towns of France, I sat with a Parisian at a variety show.

A Frenchman, with a very grubby shirt-front, presented to the audience " Señorita Pilar Naranjo, the famous dancer of Madrid." My companion started dramatically, and whispered, " I pray you to pardon me—I shall adjourn to the bar till she has done."

Of course, I followed him. " What's the matter ? "

" Do not ask me to watch her ! "

" Why ? "

" I could not support it."

" She is so bad as all that ? "

" Bad ? She is entrancing."

" Oh ! Did you see her when you were in Spain ? "

" In Paris, when I had come back. Have you read my *Sobs After Midnight* ? "

" No."

" Buy it. It contains perhaps the most poignant poems that I have written—they are moans in metres for my loss of Pilar Naranjo."

" You don't say so ? "

" She was the passion of my life." He struck an attitude. " Return to your seat alone, mon ami. For company I shall have my bitter thoughts."

Civility forbade me to let him do all the acting, himself, and I said in solemn tones, " I shall remain by your side."

He brooded heavily, with one eye on the past, and the other on the effect he was making. " In my nature," he informed me, " there is, mysteriously, some Castilian quality—no sooner had I arrived in Spain than I bore myself like a Spaniard. I spent fascinating months there, and when I came home, Paris appeared to me a foreign city. Absently I replied to people in Spanish; my fondest possession was a guitar that I had brought back. Though I could not play it, I derived exquisite pleasure from slinging it over my shoulder when I promenaded in the Garden of the Luxembourg. It may be that instinct warned my compatriots that now they were alien to me, for they seemed to avoid me, and I was alone."

" I can understand it," I said.

" One melancholy evening, as I wandered through the barren streets, pining for the magic of Granada, I noticed the name of ' Pilar Naranjo ' on the bills of a minor musique 'all. Though it was a name unknown to me, its nationality was an appeal. I entered the musique 'all. I paid for a fauteuil, and received a pink ticket. What a crisis ! Even to-day I cannot behold pink tickets without a shudder."

To the strains of an exiguous orchestra, the provocation of the lady's castanets reached our ears gaily. Her victim writhed.

" Very soon I gathered that she was popular there; but on the stage, to be a foreigner is to be a favourite, and I prepared myself to be disappointed when she appeared. Sapristi ! I was spellbound. She danced, that night, the *habenera* that she is dancing now. Ah, those cajoling arms, so irresistible ! How imperial was her form, how Southern were her feet ! And her face ! the bewildering beauty of her face that haunts me still."

I got up.

" Sit down—I could not endure your looking at her without me ! " he gasped. " When her turn finished, I had no thought but her; I was scarcely conscious of the monkeys that came next. In some fifteen minutes a girl had danced herself into my destiny—and I was swept to the stage door, like a leaf, on the gale of my emotions.

" I could see nobody inside, to take a message. Ten minutes—a quarter of an hour passed. I waited in the gloomy little cul-de-sac, dreading, in every second, to hear the approaching footstep of a rival with an appointment. So tremendous was my agitation that Spanish tenses with which I was normally familiar evaded me, and my brain buzzed with the effort to compose a preliminary phrase.

" The door opened. Before her features were visible in the darkness, the majesty of her deport-

ment proclaimed that it was she. I advanced. I
bowed, with all my grace.

" ' Señorita,' I said, ' I am a poet, and I adore
you. Will you honour me by supping with me ? '

" It was not the overwhelming eloquence that
I should have had in French, but I felt that the
fervour of my voice should make amends; and
I prayed that she would not be flippant in return.
My sentiment demanded sweet, grave, contralto
tones; a giggle would have been torture to me.
Once more, a crisis—a spiritual crisis, in which
my heart ceased to beat. Would she respond
gravely, or would she giggle ?

" *She did neither one nor the other. As if I had
not spoken, she went by.*

" *Comment donc ?* I had referred clearly to
supper; I was well-dressed, young, handsome—and
a dancer at a fifth-rate musique 'all, which was not
precisely a college for decorum, refused to dispense
with the ceremony of an introduction !

" It was prodigious. And by degrees my anger
at the affront subsided. So far from dismissing
her from my mind, I paid homage to her virtue.
Yes, my bosom was thrilled by deep esteem.
On that sad walk home, the romantic passion for
a danseuse was transmuted into a devout reverence
for a noble woman. I condemned myself for
approaching her so informally. There is, in my
complex nature, a vein of humility, extremely
winning. I resolved to write to her, confessing
my fault, before I slept.

" It was a long job, because I had to look up

so many words in a dictionary, but I foresaw
that she would be touched by the letter. In conclusion I said, ' The impulse that you scorned was
born, not of disrespect, but of an admiration,
that brooked no curb. If your vestal pride is not
adamant to my remorse, grant me, I supplicate, an
opportunity to express my penitence at the stage
door to-morrow (Wednesday).'

" Wednesday's sunshine already tinged the
street when I dropped the missive in the boite-aux-
lettres, but I was not conscious of fatigue. On the
contrary, I regretted that I must kill eighteen hours
in sleep, or some other banality, before the paradise
of her presence was attained. How much had
happened in a night ! All that was frivolous in
my disposition had passed away, and I realised
that this girl had inspired in me a devotion pro-
found, epoch-making, and supreme."

He paused. From the footlights, the Frenchman
of the dirty shirt-front was to be heard in the
capacity of interpreter : " Ladies and gentlemen,
Señorita Pilar Naranjo desires me to translate to
you her heartfelt gratitude for the enthusiasm
of your applause. If you will graciously allow her
a few moments for a change of costume, Señorita
Naranjo will have the honour of presenting to
you her sensational Toreador Dance."

The poet groaned. " When I woke I hoped to
find that I had slept well into the afternoon. With
impatience I saw that it was only mid-day. How-

ever, in dressing, I recognised that I might profit-
ably employ some of the time with the dictionary,
and I prepared a score of burning declarations
for the interview.

"The remaining hours were intolerable. No
sooner had the musique 'all opened than I took my
seat, but the exasperating entertainment appeared
to me to endure for æons before her turn. The
torments, inflicted on my suspense by a pair of
cross-talk comedians, cannot be surpassed in hell.

"At last I trembled in the cul-de-sac again.
At last she came !

"With an obeisance that consigned my career
to her feet, I murmured, ' I am here to learn whether
I am pardoned.'

"*Not a syllable ! As before, she passed me by.*

"Ah, mon Dieu ! I cannot tell you how I
reached my couch.

"But my zeal survived even this. I was stricken,
but indomitable. I said, ' Behold a saint worth
winning ! ' I said ' Brace up, and demonstrate
that you are worthy of her ! '

"My friend, every day for a month I thumbed
that exhausting dictionary, and a Spanish Grammar,
that I might send to her a sonnet every night.
For thirty days on end I wrestled with synonyms
and inversions in a foreign tongue, to create for
her a nightly proof of my genius and my love.

"And I waited for an answer vainly.

"Long after despair had mastered me, I was
with a good-for-nothing painter of my acquaintance.
He said, ' I have a new flame—delicious. Have

you heard of the Spanish dancer up at the Little Casino? '

" By a superhuman effort I controlled myself. ' Your suit prospers? '

" ' It is going strong. And only a week since I first dropped in there and saw her ! '

" ' You are a man of action ! But since when have you talked Spanish? '

" ' Oh, that isn't necessary,' he laughed; ' she is Spanish only on the stage. Between ourselves, her name is really Marie Durand—she has never been out of France in her life.'

" *She had not understood a single word that I had said, or written—and by the time I discovered it, she was another's !* He holds her still—you hear him now."

The " interpreter " was speaking again: " Señorita Naranjo desires me to translate——"

XI

THE GIRL WHO WAS TIRED OF LOVE

At the Opéra Ball, a boy had danced half the night with a partner whose youthful tones were so delicious, whose tenderness was so attractive, that he implored her a hundred times to unmask. "If I do, you'll get up and go away," she gasped at last, fondling his hand. He vowed that it was her temperament that fascinated him, and she took the mask off—and he saw the sunken face of an old, old woman.

Horrified, he left her.

In the same season, another man supplicated to a girl for her love—a girl with a face so beautiful that it made him forget the strangeness of her voice, which was flat and feeble. And the girl, who looked no more than nineteen, replied with exhaustion: "I outlived such emotions long ago. To tell you the truth, the subject sounds to me ridiculous. All I want to-day is peace and quiet."

Wearily she left him.

These two incidents, peculiar as they are, were the outcome of an occurrence queerer still—an occurrence at the tragic epoch of a woman's life when her glass says: "Stop fooling yourself. You've crumpled to *that!*"

185

Madame de Val Fleury had begun to combat the advance of age the day after she detected the first shadowy threat of crowsfeet, as she turned her perfect neck before the mirror. Her triumph was a fleeting one, and the later conquests were briefer yet. Scarcely had the enemy been driven from the glorious eyes when it crept about the chiselled nose and mouth; no sooner was its attack upon her face withheld than it showed greyly in her hair. But she never abandoned the contest, she fought with Time continuously. And although there were moods of depression, as measures more and more drastic were required, custom and vanity enabled her, year by year, decade by decade, to view her reflection with complacence. She beheld it through a haze of illusion, in applying the colour to her shrivelled cheeks. She did not note that the chestnut transformation that had looked so natural on a counter looked spurious on her head; did not see how piteously the perfect neck had sagged.

But one May morning the mirror said : " Stop fooling yourself. You've crumpled to *that !* " and madame de Val Fleury sat and saw her face withered as it was—and madame de Val Fleury wailed for her lost loveliness as she had never wailed for her dead husband and son.

A dress that she was to wear for the first time, and that had cost five thousand francs, lay on the bed. She did not glance towards it. She leant her elbows on the toilet table and stared at the brutal glass. And beyond the glass she viewed the ghost of her empire, scenes where famous beauties had turned involuntarily at her entrance. It was the women's homage, the reluctant admiration of her own sex that she mourned for, as she brooded there. In her backward gaze she saw why, as the years sped, she had squandered more and more on her modistes—saw bitterly that she had struggled to prolong, by her clothes, the fast-waning jealousy of her face.

And at Longchamp that day she knew herself to be only an old, unattractive woman, magnificently attired.

Not more than a month after this, madame de Val Fleury had the annoyance to lose a pendant sapphire that she was wearing. A reward, not illiberal, was offered, and when she woke from her nap one afternoon she was relieved to learn that the stone had been picked up by a poor girl, who was waiting in the hall to see her.

" If she is clean, I will see her here," said madame de Val Fleury.

The young girl who entered, in a threadbare frock, had been dowered with beauty so extraordinary that all the lady's pleasure at recovering her jewel was swamped in envy. The eyes, the complexion, the exquisite modelling of the features held her mute for an instant.

Subduing a sigh, she said : " I hear you have found my sapphire ? "

" Yes, madame."

" Let me look.   Where did you find it ? "

" It was in the road, madame, just against the kerb, in the rue de Berri."

"Ah, yes. I am glad you saw it. It was a piece of luck for you, too, hein?" She rose and opened her desk.

"Yes, indeed, madame," said the girl, clasping her hands.

"What are you—I mean, what do you do for a living?"

"I work at madame Wilhelmine's, madame."

"The milliner's? Why don't you go as manne-quin somewhere?—you are—er—pretty."

"They tell me my figure is not good enough, madame."

"That's true. Your figure is bad," said the lady, more amiably. "Well, you could sit to artists for the face. You could earn more money that way than Wilhelmine pays you, I should think."

"I know only one honest way to make as much money as I want, madame," said the girl, in a low voice. "I want a good deal."

"Tiens! The State lotteries, of course."

"No, madame; a likelier way than that."

"Oh! And what do you call a good deal?"

"Madame understands that I am very poor. A trifle to madame would be a good deal to *me*. Say, a hundred thousand francs."

"A hundred thousand francs! Such a sum is not a trifle to anybody. You know a way to make it?"

"Thanks to this reward, I have a chance to make it," assented the girl, folding the bank notes that had been given to her.

" And *not* the lotteries ? "

" No, madame; a journey for which I lacked the fare. But I bore madame ? "

" No, no; go on."

" Eh bien, I am sick of poverty; I would far rather part with my face and gain wealth than remain beautiful and a beggar."

" You would far rather—— What do you say ? "

" I am going to the Face Exchange, madame," said the girl resolutely.

The old woman looked at her stupefied. " The what ? " she asked in a whisper.

" Madame has not heard of it ? It is held once a year. Of course one may fail; one may not be able to strike a bargain—and even if one does, the miracle may not occur. But something tells me I shall be fortunate."

Madame de Val Fleury shrank back on the couch, frightened—she could not doubt that the girl was insane. After a moment, nerving herself to approach the bell, she stammered, " Yes, yes, I remember now. I daresay it is the best thing you can do. Good afternoon to you. I wish you every success." And as she sniffed at the smelling salts brought by her maid, she murmured, trembling, " Mad. How terrible ! Quite, quite mad."

The incident did not fade from her mind. She thought of it in the night, and on the morrow, and when she took the sapphire and the snapped chain to her jeweller's. If the nonsense the poor creature talked had only been true ! What ecstasy ! And her tone had been perfectly sane.

. . . Oh, of course she was demented. Still—
still, miracles did happen. Look at Lourdes!
Every day madame de Val Fleury recalled the
matter with a curiosity more intense, and regretted
the alarm that had prevented her obtaining details.

Before a week had gone by, the curiosity drove
her to make a purchase at the milliner's the girl
had mentioned.

" You have a young person employed here who
found a jewel that I lost," she remarked. " I
don't see her in the shop."

" Yes, madame. No, madame—she is in the
workroom. How fortunate that madame's sapphire
was restored to her ! "

" Ah, the workroom. Have you had her long?
Is she satisfactory ? "

" Ah yes, madame. About two years. I have
no fault to find with her."

" I fancied she was a little odd in her manner.
You have not noticed anything of the kind ? "

" Mais non, madame. No doubt she was shy
in madame's presence. No, she is quick to take
a hint, that girl; she has all her wits about
her."

" You might tell her I should like to have a
word with her," faltered madame de Val Fleury.
And when the girl appeared, still more beautiful
without a hat, she said, " Come to my flat again
this evening about nine o'clock if you can. I will
make it worth your while. I want to talk to
you."

As she passed out she felt breathless and dizzy.

"Then, if she is not mad—" panted madame de Val Fleury, "then, if she is not mad—— My God, can there be something in it?"

She had been going to a neighbour's for a game of écarté after dinner, and écarté was a passion with her, but she knew no regrets in cancelling the engagement. A book by her favourite novelist, just published, lay to hand, and reading was another of her pet pleasures, but she did not open it, as she sat waiting for the hour to strike. Punctually at nine o'clock the bell rang. The girl was shown in.

"Good evening," said madame de Val Fleury. "Sit down. No, no, not so far off. Come closer. Tell me. I have been wondering. . . . What you were speaking about the other afternoon. Is it really a fact?"

"Madame means my intention?"

"I mean the place itself. It actually exists?"

"Ah, certainly it exists, madame!"

"Where is it?"

"In Brittany, madame. Near Pont Chouay."

"But—it sounds incredible! I am sure you are sincere, but—how long have you known of it?"

"I have known of it ever since the first miracle that happened there, madame, four years ago. I lived in the village then. The face of a little girl, the miller's child, was burnt—ah, it was frightful to see!—and her mother knelt and prayed, the whole night through, that she herself might bear the scars instead. And at dawn it *was* so, and the child's face was as fair as ever."

" It takes one's breath away ! What is the village called ? "

" St. Pierre des Champs, madame. If madame goes there and inquires, everyone will confirm what I tell her."

" And such miracles have happened again ? "

" At dawn on each seventh of September, madame. I assure madame I speak the truth."

" Listen," said madame de Val Fleury. " I shall go and hear what they say. If I am satisfied, are you willing to—to exchange your face for mine ? I will not haggle with you, I will pay what you want. It is a large amount, but you shall have it— a hundred thousand francs."

" One would have to think over the price, madame," said the girl hesitatingly.

" What ? It is the figure you named."

" Yes—for an exchange. But it is possible I might change with someone of my own years. Naturally I should prefer that."

" You do not suppose a young girl would pay a hundred thousand francs ? " cried madame de Val Fleury, wincing. " If she has youth already, what for ? "

" For beauty. There are many young girls who would be content to do so."

" There will not be many living in a little village."

" Ah, madame, people who know arrive from all parts. Besides, it might be better for me to take even fifty thousand francs with a young face than a hundred thousand with—with one more mature. Madame understands that I am human—

I am not indifferent to the other sex.   If I sacrifice
all my prospects of admiration, sweethearts,
husband, it is worth a great sum."

" I shall go and hear what they say," repeated
madame de Val Fleury, deeply mortified.   " What
is your name? "

" Berthe Cheron, madame."

" Put it down for me, and your private address.
If what I hear convinces me perhaps we may come
to terms."

All night the old woman dreamt she was again
of surpassing loveliness, the envy of all the women
of her world.

She went to Brittany the same week, and
returned palpitating with the tales that had been
told her.   She agreed with mademoiselle Cheron
to pay 120,000 francs if the metamorphosis occurred,
and it was arranged that, when the time came, they
should travel to St. Pierre des Champs together.

In the meanwhile her rapturous reflections were
not free from anxiety.   If the dawning of the longed-
for date should indeed yield her Berthe Cheron's
face, she would be no longer recognised as madame
de Val Fleury.   Her social circle would not know
her; monsieur Septfous, her banker—she banked
at a private bank, and monsieur Septfous was
practically her man of business—would not know
her; her servants themselves would not know
her when she came back to Paris.   To explain
would be to meet with perpetual embarrassments.
On the whole, the best plan would be to change
her name as well.   It would mean relinquishing

o

a few friendships that she valued, but—— Again,
she foresaw herself dazzlingly fair, and caught her
breath.   Her loveliness would compensate a million-
fold.

Her income was derived chiefly from Municipal
Bonds and Métro shares.   At the bank she had
also a substantial sum on deposit.   She told
monsieur Septfous that she had decided to spend
the rest of her life in the country, and she took a
draft, payable to bearer, for the full amount of
cash, and removed her box of securities.

She determined to call herself madame de
Beaulieu.

Late on the evening of the 6th of September
the old woman and the girl arrived at St. Pierre des
Champs.

They had expected to arrive earlier, but the
train crept into Pont Chouay at 7.30 instead of
5.15, and thence they were dependent on the local
fiacres, which were hard to find and slow to move.
Madame de Val Fleury reached the village, impatient
and fatigued.

In the little moonlit market-place, with its
vacant stalls, when they entered it at last, many
figures circulated, scrutinising one another's features
eagerly.   Most of the men and women bore lanterns,
and one of the stalls had evidently been sub-let
for the evening; under the sign " Christophe :
Cheese, Eggs, and Butter," a humpback had
electric torches for sale.   As the pair made their
way, across the cobbles, to the shrine that had been
erected beside the water-mill, no face of much

beauty met their view. The sellers appeared to
be chiefly buxom peasant girls, wholesome looking,
but no more. Those who had come to buy were
of types more various. Here, an old roué, fraudu-
lently dyed and painted, peered avidly at the features
of a youth, who raised his lantern and rebuffed
him with a jeer. There, an individual with crafty
lips and predatory eyes, obviously a sharper, was
to be seen bargaining for the physiognomy of a
simpleton. A man with a round humorous face
darted each moment from one melancholy counten-
ance to another, and a passer-by said, loud enough
to be overheard : " Look at Jibily, the low comedian
—he is crazy to play tragic parts ! " Irritating
and incessant was the shrill outcry of a female
broker, hobbling with a file of maids-of-all-work
at her heels. " Fine faces cheap ! " clamoured the
crone. " Fine faces cheap ! "

It became very cold beside the water-mill. As
the laggard night wore by, madame de Val Fleury
shivered distressfully. Alternately she prayed and
despaired. More than once she glanced, tense with
hope, at her companion, striving to detect some
promise of the sought-for change, but the girl's
face remained unaltered. In the serene radiance
of the moon its fairness was exquisite beyond words,
and the woman wrung her hands with the intensity
of her desire.

Slowly, slowly the moonlight faded. The pallor
of dawn streaked the sky; and a hundred faces
were upturned beseechingly, a hundred suppliants
trembled. Wan and white grew the scene. A

tremor and a rustling stirred the huddled figures. Suddenly, somewhere a woman wailed, " No use ! " and burst into sobs. Berthe Cheron, fearful now the moment had come, of beholding herself gaunt-cheeked and wrinkled, bowed her head, shuddering, in her hands. Madame de Val Fleury, half dazed with exhaustion and suspense, bent to the shining surface of the pool. The pool receded. It became suddenly unreal. Next, her pounding heart was squeezed with terror—she didn't know if the reflection she beheld was her own, or Berthe Cheron's, from behind her. She nodded wildly at her reflection; she grimaced and gesticulated at it, like a madwoman. . . . It had happened ! She thought she gave an ear-piercing shriek of joy, but she fainted, without a sound.

After the money was paid she neither saw nor heard anything of Berthe Cheron. Aided by a lady whose birth gave her the passport to society, and whose income made her amenable to a financial offer, madame de Val Fleury, or, as she now called herself, Victorine de Beaulieu, was the sensation of Paris that autumn. The consummate toilettes permitted by her wealth lent to her face a beauty even more transcendent than Berthe Cheron's had been. When she drove, people pressed forward on the sidewalks to regard her. When she entered her box at the Opera, everybody in the house to whom the box was visible looked at her as much as at the stage. In salons, faces the most admired before her advent paled in her presence, like candle flames in sunshine. She was paramount and she revelled in the knowledge. Yet the transformation had its lack. She missed her game of écarté with her erstwhile neighbour. She missed the garrulity of familiar friends whom she no longer met. There were hours when, despite the transports afforded by the mirror now, she found time hang heavy on her hands. And the hands, of course, had not recovered girlishness and beauty. Nor her body, nor her mind.

That was the drawback. Only her face was young. Physically and mentally she was old. Her corsetière could not provide her with a figure to match the face. Her physician could not give back to her the energies that had gone. Her mirror itself was impotent to revive the enthusiasm and illusions of her youth.

Men made love to the bewildering " young widow." After the first thrill of amazed exultance she was bored. Their fervour kindled no responsive spark. Her aged heart beat no faster. The sentiment, the rhapsodies poured into her ear seemed drearily stupid to the old woman, as she posed on balconies, wishing she were in her bedroom with a cup of tisane and her slippers. During the third passionate proposal addressed to her, it was with extreme difficulty that she restrained her jaws from yawning.

" Why are you so cold—why won't you hear me ? " men cried to her. And she answered dully : " I am not impressionable. It doesn't interest me to be made love to. I am tired of all that."

And she was spoken of in Paris as the " girl who was tired of love."

Many evenings during the winter there were when the knowledge that she would be wearied by some man's appeal, if she went out, determined her to remain at home. The opportunity to out-shine other women failed to lure her from the fireside, and she sat in her dressing-gown, playing écarté with her new maid.   " It is marvellous what a head for the game madame has, seeing she is so young ! " exclaimed the maid, awestruck. " I cannot say as much for *you*," snapped her mistress, mourning that quondam neighbour.

When the summer came and she went to the coast, with a score of wonderful dresses, she sighed for companionship more drearily yet. Hitherto, at such places, she had sat among her compeers, amiably chatting. Now she appeared too young to be congruous to the circle of the old—was too old to participate in the pastimes of the young. Scant of breath and stiff in the joints, she viewed morosely the laughing women trooping to the tennis courts. Shrunken beneath her youthful frocks, she dared not don a bathing costume and reveal her wasted form among the sirens lolling by the tents. Queer as the fact seemed, her years irked her more this summer than they had done while she looked her age.

The anniversary of the miracle found her in low spirits, and suffering from lumbago.

There was a lad, attractive, promising, on the threshold of a career—such a lad as, thirty-eight

years earlier, she had pictured her baby growing
up to be. She had made his acquaintance at a
" feeve o'clock," where, being so young, he felt shy,
and where to find himself speaking to this enchant-
ress confused him more still. But her tone had
promptly relieved him of his dread that he ought
to play the courtier. When she invited him to
call on her, she asked him as she might have asked
a schoolboy. Her interest in Guy Verne's ambitions
yielded to her gradually a healthier outlook.
Stranger still, as the months passed, a real and deep
affection stole into the old egoist's nature. She
was less purposeless, less futile for it. Almost,
as she entered into his boyish forecasts, and made
light of his little setbacks, it seemed to her as if
her son had lived.

One day the boy flung his arms round her and
begged her to be his wife.

It was horrible. She repulsed him, shuddering.
" Don't, Guy, don't ! "

Entreaties poured from him.

" If you understood ! " she moaned. " I shall
have gone to my grave while you're a young
man."

He thought she meant that she was very ill.
" I'll nurse you back to health. Victorine, I love
you with all my soul."

" You don't love me a bit," she said. " There
is nothing in me for you to love—I am as utterly
different from you as if there were fifty years
between us ; you only imagine you love me because
you admire my face. Good heavens, have I ever

said a single word to lead you to think I cared for you in such a way? "

An English boy might have suffered as much, but would have taken it more quietly. This boy was French, and he did not hide what he felt. He answered vehemently that she had led him to think so every time they talked of his future. " If you didn't care for me, why should it interest you? " He raved of his broken heart. He loaded her with reproaches. " You've shammed to me, mocked me, just to amuse yourself ! "

" No." She was crying. " I *am* fond of you— fonder of you than of anybody in the world. But not like that. I shall never care like that again for anyone."

" I wish I had never seen you. I wish I were dead."

" You mustn't come here any more," she found the strength to tell him—and not till then had she realised how very dear he had become to her. " I'm so sorry, Guy—so dreadfully sorry."

He fell at her feet, imploring her anew. He broke down, and besought one kiss before he left her. Her misery was deeper than his as she bent to him, but the boy didn't know it.

" My God," he sobbed, " I adore you—and you kiss me as if you were my mother ! "

The mirror provided no comfort in her loss. She stared, lonely, at the alien face reflected— stared at it, by slow degrees, with aversion. It was not she. The unlovely form and jaded mind were she—the spent passion, and the infirmities.

What benefit was the face of youth without youth's pulses? The mirror mocked her weary thoughts each day.

Upon her grief a woman, white-lipped and shaken, intruded to upbraid her.

" You have ruined my son's career," she said. " He neglects his work, he thinks of nothing but you. I hope and pray you may be punished as you deserve ! "

" At Guy's age a career is not ruined by a foolish attachment," pleaded madame de Val Fleury piteously.

" And at yours such an answer is abominable," cried the other. " You do not lessen your guilt by cynicism. If ever a girl encouraged a young man, you encouraged my son. Foolish as his devotion to you may be, he *is* devoted to you. By what right did you tempt him to come here constantly if you had no tenderness for him? Your treatment of him has been infamous."

" As a mother, do you know only one kind of tenderness, madame? My affection for your son was true and great. My interest in his future was no less deep than yours. I swear to you that what has happened distresses me so much that I have been able to think of nothing else."

Madame Verne advanced upon her with clenched hands.

" Your hypocrisy is even more revolting than your cynicism. If I know more than one kind of tenderness? Yes. But not in a girl for a young man ! You swear to me you are distressed. *I*

swear to *you* something else.   My boy is all I have
—and I am frightened for him; I do not know
what he may do in his despair. If I lose him he
shall be revenged.   Take care, madame de Beaulieu. If you hear of his death, take care! The
very next day, if possible, or the next month, or
the next year—whenever I can reach you—as
Heaven is my witness, I will mark that face of yours
with vitriol."

She rang the bell, and went—and the maid that
entered found her mistress in a swoon upon the
floor.

For a week her shattered nerves kept madame
de Val Fleury abed.   And for several weeks terror
prevented her from setting foot outside the flat.
She had a grille constructed in the door, and a
hundred times she repeated to the servants that
it was not to be opened for the merest instant to
madame Verne, or any stranger. Such precautions
could not yield composure, however. The day
was rendered ghastly with false alarms; and when
she glanced at the mirror, dread flared upon her
now a face seared and repulsive, a mutilated, sightless thing of horror. The night brought dreams
so fearful that she was, more than once, wakened
by a scream that had burst from her. Thrice
the awfulness of the tension impelled her to falter,
through the telephone, sympathetic and ingratiating inquiries to madame Verne; and when the
mother rang off without vouchsafing a reply, the
poor old creature tottered with panic.

At last, towards the close of February, she had the

unspeakable relief of learning that madame Verne
and her son had gone to Monaco, and once again
she was able to step into her car with a sense of
safety. Nevertheless, the thought of the unhappiness that she had brought upon the boy was black
in her mind. She tried to thrust the thought
aside by reading, but fiction had lost its power
to charm her. Gradually, as her health improved,
she turned, for respite from her sad reflections,
to the theatre. When there remained no more
fashionable programmes for her to see, she would
adventure the second-rate. One night, as she was
coming out of a little theatre in the Montmartre
quarter, she started and stopped short, trembling
in every limb at a sight that met her gaze.
She could not withdraw her gaze—she was mag-
netised by the sight; it thrilled her as if the dead
had risen to her view. She was looking at the
face that had been hers—she was looking at
Berthe Cheron.

Berthe Cheron, handsomely dressed, had also
jerked to a standstill, and for a few seconds the
two fronted each other dumbly—the young girl's
puckered eyes, her furrowed cheeks rancorous with
regret. It was she who was the first to speak.

" Blast you ! " she said.

" What do you mean—I treated you fairly,
didn't I ? " stammered madame de Val Fleury.

" I wish—I wish——" Resentment choked her.

" I paid all you wanted."

" Paid ? It wouldn't have been good enough
if you'd paid a million. *You* knew—*you* knew

who was getting the best of it. Paid? What's the use of the money without any fun? Do you think fine clothes make up for that? I want to be danced with, I want to be kissed. To hell with your money—I want love ! "

" Don't talk so loudly, don't! That man's looking at us."

" He's not looking at *me*. No man ever looks at me. Paid? If we were both as we were, you could pay some other fool—it wouldn't be me you'd get ! "

" If we were both as we were, I'd pay no one," groaned madame de Val Fleury.

" What? "

" It's true. Quite, quite true."

For a moment they were silent again, studying each other. Then madame de Val Fleury said breathlessly :

" I want to ask you something. Come home with me—get into my car. Don't abuse me any more, don't rail at me—I'm an old woman and I can't bear it."

As the car bore them away, she explained herself, weeping.

" I know it seems strange to you, my not being satisfied—I know I've got the things you want so much. But *you* retain the capacity to enjoy those things, and *I don't*. If I could have had your youth as well, it would have been different. The old are happiest in their old ways, with their old friends. We both made an error. If—do you think, if we were to go there again——? "

Berthe Cheron turned to her wildly. "If we were to go there again?" she gasped.

"If we were to go there again—in humbleness of spirit this time, in contrition, beseeching pardon for our error—do you think it might be undone?"

"Oh, let us try, let us try!" cried the girl, seizing her hand. And she, too, wept. "But I could not refund more than about half the money," she faltered, dismayed.

"I would not ask you to refund a sou of it," said madame de Val Fleury. "You should keep it as a marriage portion."

In the flat they talked till late, mingling their tears and comforting each other.

Nearly four months had to pass before the coming of the date they craved, but on the evening of the 6th of September the two victims of their own folly reached St. Pierre des Champs once more. And in the eerie market-place, the lanterns swayed amid the flitting figures, and again they heard the shrill clamour of the crone, shuffling among the naked stalls. "Fine faces cheap!" And the long, long night grew cold, and the penitents' teeth chattered; and as the elder knelt and prayed, as never had she prayed before, the pebbles bit into her knees.

A few days afterwards, monsieur Septfous, in the private office of the bank, saw the door open to admit a caller that surprised him.

"My dear madame de Val Fleury," he exclaimed,

" how delighted I am to greet you ! Dare I hope you have returned to Paris for good ? "

" For good, my friend—the country got on my nerves. At my time of life not every change is desirable," replied the old lady, beaming.

And subsequently one man said to another :

" Funny thing; at Bullier last night I saw a girl just like madame de Beaulieu, who vanished to New York or somewhere—excepting that she had her arms round a chap's neck and looked so happy."

" Lucky chap, by Jove ! Know him ? "

" A fellow called Guy Verne."

XII

IN THE YEAR OF OUR LORD 1918

Dear Nelly,

I was in the theatre last night, just to have a look at you again, and I saw you when you came out of the stage door. Saw the toff and the taxi waiting to take you to supper. Wonder if you can call my name to mind any more? Alf. Alf that was your sweetheart when you were in the fancy department at Skinner and Mopham's. Loved you true, I did.

Remember the early closing days when we used to go to the theatre together, Nelly? Remember *me* taking you to supper at the ham and beef shop four years ago? Wouldn't set foot in the ham and beef shop now, would you? No class. But I've been fair sick with longing for the sight of it, myself, since the day I joined up, and you cried in the City Road, with your arms round my neck. Bright as heaven it looked, the gas shining on all the sausages, when I was all over lice in the line, with my jaws chattering. Thought of it just as I was going over the top once. Saw the chap in his white jacket, cutting a sandwich and smearing the mustard on. Saw him plain.

Bit I read in a London paper over there said the

" pre-war time, now it had passed away, seemed
like an evil dream." It didn't seem like that to
me. The " bad old days of peace," the paper called
it. Said all us boys would " find it painful to go
back to business, after the great romance and glory
of war." I *don't* think. I know one of them that
would have given something to be back, calling
" Sign," in the bad old days of peace, while he was
sticking that great romance. Made me feel funny
all over to see London again at last, and look at
the " civilian population that was bearing their
trials with such heroic fortitude." Too good to
be true it felt, till I got a mouthful of what they
call beer in this better world I hear we've made,
and found the lord duke behind the bar treating
me as if I was dirt. Made me wonder if paying
sixpence for half a pint was asking for charity.
Seem to have forgotten how to be civil, all the
publicans, now it's the law for them to loaf the best
part of the day, and make you pay so that they
do as well in one week as they used to do in three.
That's what I'm told by a chap, whose uncle has
got a pub—the profit on one week's loafing is about
the same as it was on three weeks' work. Done too
well in the shops to be civil, too, I notice,
while I've been freezing and bleeding in that there
great romance. It's " Hope the war lasts for ever,"
isn't it? Mother couldn't bear to go out, because
of what the neighbours are saying. People with
sons of their own, too. It makes me wonder who
I've been doing it for. There's mother—and there
used to be you. Makes me wonder about lots of

things, religion and that. At church, on Sunday, the collection was for teaching our Christianity to the heathen, the peaceful heathen that aren't busy bombing one another. And nobody laughed.

Don't make any mistake. I'm not saying England hadn't got to fight. England had got to fight, right enough, because it ain't a civilised world. But the parsons, and the priests, and the rabbis, and the papers could have said how horrible it was, our not having learnt any way to settle things, ever since we took to wearing clothes, except new ways of slaughtering one another. They hadn't got to pretend war was something fine, and splendid, and improving. They hadn't got to pretend war had changed every woman in England to a holy angel, and Englishmen were " finding their souls " by driving bayonets through other men's bellies. England couldn't help going to war, but England could have helped praising war. We were told, at the start, as how Armageddon had been led up to by those German writers that had " preached the devilish doctrine " that war did good. They must have had a rare job, if they preached it more than our own newspapers were preaching it before a month was up. Those of them that *I* saw, anyhow. If the war has been such an " ennobling influence," if it has " purified " us all half, or a quarter as much as they keep on saying, the Kaiser must be the best benefactor England ever had. Then why don't they put up a monument to him in Trafalgar Square?

And what did they want to put the " Great

P

War " for on the shrines I see? I should have
thought they might have found a better word for
it than " great." Ain't " great " bringing up the
kids to hold with the lie that war is an ennobling
influence, like the savages do? If I had *my* way,
I'd put the " Cruelest War," or the " Worst War "
on all the shrines.

Remember how I used to hate Gus Hooper for
his conscientious objector lay? Well, I'm not keen
on him now—Hooper may have been a swine—but
I've come to see that, if war is ever done away
with, it will be just because the real conscientious
objectors are top dog. I expect by then they won't
be called conscientious objectors, and it will sound
strange to read how, in our time, there weren't
more than a few men or women that didn't think
it a virtue to commit murder if you put on khaki.
Even ladies you can't say too much for—I mean,
real ladies, not our disgraceful sort, them that
have been heroines, a lot of them, and worked themselves to shadows—I've heard more than one of
them put in a good word for war, with " They say
war brings out men's best qualities." You could
hear that, under their pity for us, they approved of
war. It did come on me as a shock. I used to
think we were all so up-to-date, all the finished
article, if you know what I mean. I don't think
anybody will look the same to me again, quite, no
matter how smart they are dressed. When you
look at people in the streets now, you can
often fancy them as Ancient Britons, coming
along naked. There's nothing that looks quite

the same. Not sunshine in the parks. You cheer up wonderful, for a minute, and then you feel as if the sunshine was *camouflage*, too. War won't ever be done away with because kaisers and governments leave off wishing they could grab something that somebody else has grabbed first—it isn't in human nature—but only because they can't get men willing to kill, and be mangled for it. " Civilised warfare " ? Might as well talk about Peaceful massacre. Why, if this bloody world of ours was civilised, there'd have been no need for England to go to war, or Belgium to go to war, or anybody else to go to war. No need for Fritz to go to war. We shouldn't have had the Worst War at all. Bill, and his war gang would have been seized by the Germans themselves, and clapped into gaol, or a lunatic asylum, according to what the doctors said about them.

Went over to Skinner and Mopham's, hoping to find you. They haven't done so bad, neither, with their heroic fortitude. I'm told the girls that used to run in for six-three-farthing quills for their hats have been buying separation allowance coats at thirty guineas as fast as hands could pick them off the hooks. Still, Mopham passed the time of day with me quite familiar, considering. " Proud thought for a young fellow that he's done his duty to his country," he says. " Only wish I'd been of military age, myself," he says. " See our Roll of Honour in the window ? Framed very stylish, I think. Spared no expense to make it a handsome article. What for you, miss ? Furs, forward ! "

It was there that I heard you had gone wrong. " The women are splendid ! " What price the rest ? Made me feel queer last night, being so close to you again, Nelly, though you didn't recognise the bit of my face that the bandages let you see. I was the cripple by the door of the taxi, when you and the toff got in.

ALF.

XIII

A POT OF PANSIES

THIS afternoon it chanced that three men, who used to be firm friends, were all sitting in the Café de la Paix at the same time. They pretended not to notice one another. And to-night my thoughts keep reverting to a pot of pansies, the pot of pansies that was so great a power.

I exaggerate nothing. It is I, Pierre Camus, pressman, who affirm it.

Jacques Rouelle still struggled as a writer of short stories, and Henri Dufour was already succeeding as a playwright, but they remained as cordial as ever. No jealousy on the one side, nor pomposity on the other. Their wives, too, were on affectionate terms; in fact, the women were cousins. As for me, I was the comrade of them all. In their modest flat—a great name for two rooms— Jacques and Blanche Rouelle would read to me manuscripts, and bewail the terms Jacques got for them; and in their little villa, off the rue Pergolèse, Henri and Elise Dufour would talk to me of some comedy that Henri was perpending, and even confide to me their discomfiture when he had one declined. Two devoted couples; five ardent friends. And then, by a stroke of fate, Jacques discovered the pot of pansies!

I had gone to see him one day, and found that he was out. Blanche, however, was at home, and Elise had just dropped in, bringing a toy or something for the child. Very charming and fashionable she looked, though I knew her well enough to be sure she had put on one of her shabbiest costumes for the visit. She told us that Henri had begun the penultimate act of the play on which he had been at work ever since the spring, and that he had talked of it recently to Martime, who was much attracted by the thesis. She was in high feather, and her elation was natural. Martime had produced an earlier piece of Henri's, but that had been no guarantee that he would like this one, and I knew that Henri's heart was set on his playing the leading part.

" Mind you don't forget to send Jacques and me tickets for the dress rehearsal," said Blanche blithely.

" As if we were likely to forget you ! Or Pierre either," said the other, smiling to me. " Of course we don't know yet that Martime will do the piece, but he was so enthusiastic about the theme, and his part is so good, that we're pretty confident. I daresay he will want some silly alterations made, but I don't think there's much doubt about his taking it, when it's ready."

" How lovely to be able to write for the theatre ! " Blanche exclaimed. " Think, all the money Jacques has had from editors, with his royalties from *Contes du Quartier* as well, is not anything like as much as Henri can make with a single play ! " And, as if fearing that her cousin might misconstrue her plaint, she added emotionally, " Not that I grudge him his good fortune, Heaven knows ! "

" I know it, too, chérie," responded Elise, squeezing her hand. " Jacques' innings will come. I am very sure it will come. It is atrocious that Henri and I should have all the luck in the meantime."

The vivacity seemed to be taking a solemn turn, so I put in, " And what about *me* ? For me both your households are too wealthy—I blunder in knowing either of you. A pauper should never have rich friends."

" Tiens ! That is a novel philosophy," said Elise inquiringly.

" It is sound. What do they yield him? At best, an invitation to dinner. Which does not compensate for the despondence he suffers in contrasting their grandeur with his garret. The poor devil of discretion associates with people even worse off than himself—and by comparison feels prosperous."

" You old humbug ! " they laughed at me. And addressing Blanche again, Elise Dufour said, " Wait till those dividends come rolling in ! He will gnash his teeth more than ever, won't he ? "

" Dividends ? " said I. " What dividends ? Who dares to mention dividends in front of me ? "

" Ah ! he hasn't heard," cried Blanche, recovering her buoyancy. " Henri is going to get a hundred shares for Jacques in a company that is coming out.

We should not be able to get them ourselves, but
the man is a friend of Henri's.   What do you think
of it, our making investments ?   Isn't it great ? "

" It is true," said Elise, nodding.   " It will be a
very good thing.   Henri means to apply for quite
a lot."

I could guess what it was, though, not being a
capitalist, I paid no heed to the Bourse and was
absolutely ignorant whether Amalgamated Pan-
cakes were heavy, or Funded Fireworks had gone
up.   Henri had chanced to speak of it to me.   I
had no doubt that Jacques might do much worse
than hold a hundred shares in that concern.

" What do you think of it ? " repeated Blanche.
" We have been working eight years to save three
thousand francs—won't it seem wonderful to have
a few francs that we haven't worked for at all
coming in every year ? "

She went on talking about it after Elise had
gone.   " It will be like something in a fairy tale,
to have a little money falling regularly to us from
the skies, as it were.   What it will mean !   Even
Henri and Elise do not know.   We shall be in a
position to indulge in pleasures that sound fantastic
now.   For instance, if Jacques is out of sorts, I
shall be able to pack him off to the country to get
well.   To-day he would not hear of such a thing—
he would not touch our nest-egg if he were on his
last legs.   And the little one !   What joy to buy
Baby's clothes without dipping into that !   To
buy him perhaps a little fur coat out of money that
poor Jacques has not had to whip his brains for.

Won't he look sweet, the pet, dressed in dividends?
I wish that *you* could take some shares, Pierre.
But I know."

Then Jacques returned, seemingly deep in
thought, and I said : " Come in and make
yourself at home. Congratulations, my financial
magnate ! "

" Hein ? " he queried. " What? Oh, that !
Yes. It had slipped my mind for the moment."
He went over to his wife and kissed her tenderly.
It appeared that he had been out for two or three
hours, and he demanded, with deep anxiety, if the
child still thrived.

" Mais oui, goose. He sleeps in there," said
Blanche. " The shares had slipped thy mind?
Ah, but listen, thou dwellest overmuch on thy
work—in the end thou wilt have a breakdown."

" But no, but no, little woman. On the contrary,
never have I felt more fit. I have just seen something that is positively inspiring," he announced.
" I have seen a suggestion for a short story that is
exquisite."

" So ? " We were all attention.

" Quite by accident. I had been walking aim-
lessly, wandering without noting where I turned,
when in the twilight I found myself in a long street
of decay that struck a chill to my heart. The
slatternly, forbidding houses had an air of hope-
lessness, of evil that made me shudder. I tried to
classify the denizens, but well as I know Paris, I
was baffled. I had the impression of entering a
street of mysteries. It was as if, behind each of

those morose, darkling windows, lowering upon me
in their hundreds, there lurked gruesome things.
Suddenly, on the foul ledge of a ground-floor
window, dim with dirt, behind which some nameless
stuff was looped, further to hide the secrets of the
room, I saw blooming—a pot of pansies! I cannot
tell you how infinitely fresh its fairness looked in
these surroundings, how divinely incongruous!
I stood gazing at it a full minute, lost in conjecture.
Who, in that sinister house, retained the sensibility
to tend a pot of pansies? What message did it
yield her? How did she come to be there? 'Mon
Dieu,' I said, ' a story! A great story!' I was
enraptured. When I reached a decent quarter,
I sat down on a bench, and lit a cigarette, and
prepared to welcome the delicious plot that I foresaw emerging from my reverie."

"Tell it to us," we begged him.

The fervour of Jacques' tones abated. They
were flat when he replied.

"Strange to say, it did not emerge," he said.
"I have not been able to find it yet."

"It will arrive," we cried, with conviction.
"There should be an excellent story in that."

"Ah, certainly it will arrive. My only misgiving is that I am not worthy to treat it. It should
be a gem, that story, a masterpiece. It should be
a story that will live. . . . All the same, it piques
me that, with such a stimulus to write, I should
have to wait, even for an hour. I am athirst to
begin."

"You will strike the idea before you go to bed,"

I assured him. " Even I, though fiction is not my line, can see a story there."

" You can see it ? " he inquired eagerly.

" I do not mean that I see the plot. But I see the prospects."

" Ah, yes, that is how it is with *me*," he said. " The prospects are magnificent, aren't they? What delight I shall take in this ! I may not be capable of handling it as well as it deserves, but you are going to see the best short story I have ever done, mon vieux."

Well, changes in the staff transferred me abruptly to London soon after that, and I had no further conversation on the subject with Jacques till nearly five months had passed. The interval had threatened to be longer still, but one must eat. Why can't you cut an English cook's throat? If you don't know the answer you are unaware that in England they placidly consume anything that is put on their plates. Because there are no English cooks. I should like frequently to sojourn in the beautiful countryside of England, if it were not so painful to see vegetables growing there. When I looked at those verdant young things, so full of flavour and nutriment, and thought of the fate before them—reflected that they were destined to be drowned in hogsheads of water, and served as an unpalatable pulp, the sight of them used to wring my heart. I overtook Jacques in the Champs Élysées one day, as I was on my way to call on Henri and Elise, and we strolled along together. I said : " I rather thought you would send me a copy of that story you were speaking of before I went. What paper was it published in ? "

To my amazement, he replied gloomily : " It is not written. I am seeking the plot for it."

" What ? " I exclaimed. " Not written ? After five months ? If you could turn out other stories in the meantime, why not that one ? "

" I have not turned out other stories in the meantime," he told me. " I am concentrating my imagination on the pot of pansies."

I stopped and stared at him. " Ah, ça ! Are you in earnest ? Mon Dieu ! It looked very promising, but if you mean to spend the rest of your life trying to write it, the promise will cost you dear."

" I know it is unpractical of me," he owned distressfully. " I have eaten up a pretty penny. I reproach myself. But the fascination is overwhelming. I cannot withstand it. The thing has become an obsession. I have been back a dozen times, in all weathers, to look at the house again. But the course has not advanced me. In desperation, I even rang the bell and asked to see the occupant of that room, but the crone who opened the street-door was either so deaf, or so artful, that it was impossible to make her understand what I said. Let us talk about it ! There are only three points to resolve. Who, in a house like that, has still the sensibility to tend a pot of pansies ? What does it say to her ? By what circumstances is she there ? "

" I remember, I remember," I said. " I am

not provided with answers to such conundrums at any moment of the day. But I could have answered them in less than five months, I'll swear." I added, " If you like, I will find the plot for you, in a quarter of an hour, some time, when I have nothing else to do." I did not mean it very seriously, and, of course, I am a busy man.

At this juncture, we saw Henri approaching— a deuce of a swell in his frock-overcoat and chamois gloves, though his figure was more protruberant than it had been in the period when he was among the Great Unacted. He hailed us with : " You rascals, you negligent knaves ! If you greet me once in a century, it is by chance. How are you, darlings ? "

" We meant to honour you with a visit now," I said. " As it is, we will go on and see Elise. Come back and see her too."

" Elise has gone to a matinée," said Henri. " You shall take a little ta-ta with me, instead. I am on topping terms with myself, and need some-one to listen to my boasts. I read my play to Martime this week. All is well. When I finished, tears were in his eyes."

" Good business ! " We exulted hardly less than he.

" When will it be seen ? " asked Jacques. " Will he make it his next production ? "

" Ah, that is not settled. For that matter, he has not actually agreed to take it. But he has got the script, and he is to write to me in a few days. I know well enough what is going to happen ; I shall have to agree that the leading woman's part ought to be less strong. And then he will tell me the play is flawless."

" You do not mind sacrificing her ? "

" If I mind ? Well, naturally I mind. Mais que voulez-vous ? My primary desire is Martime. His vanity is colossal, but it is a man's play, and no other actor on the stage could do what *he* will do with it. I constructed it for him from the start. You may be sure I will make concessions rather than lose Martime. Ah, we are rejoicing ! This piece means a great deal to us, you know—it is ambitious work. With this, if it succeeds, I—en effet, I am promoted to the front rank."

" You are not at the foot of the class now," I said.

" Ah ! But I have written for fees rather than for fame. It was not good enough to clothe my wife and children in rags because I aspired to wear laurels. The day I entreated Elise to marry a boy who had not five hundred francs, I was guilty of a crime. I have never forgotten the confidence she showed in me that day—nor her unwavering belief in me while times were bad. In truth, my wife has but one failing—she admires me to excess. According to her, every word I write, or speak, is inspired. But it is not odious to be worshipped. She is adorable. I ask myself what I should do without her. They may say some of the pieces I have done so far are of no account; I assure you I have had far more joy from scribbling a farce that bought smart costumes or a bracelet for Elise than I could have had from evolving classics that left her worried about the washing bill. Enfin, everything comes at last to him who waits—even a fine day in London, hein?—and now I have felt entitled to devote twelve months to a grand attempt. And, if it is well received—I do not romance when I say that, if it is well received, the thing that will make me proudest will be the admiration of my dear wife."

While he talked on, opening his heart to us, we strode towards the Boulevard; and as we proceeded to the Boulevard, with never a premonition of disaster, it is not hyperbolic to affirm that all Paris would have failed to display a trio more united.

Presently he inquired of Jacques: " Anything wrong with you? You are very quiet."

" I search for a plot," sighed our friend; and was long-winded.

" He has been able to think of nothing but the enchanting story that ought to blossom from that flower-pot, and doesn't," I explained. " By this time he might have——"

" The points I ponder are three," Jacques broke in strenuously. " Who, in such environment, has the lingering sensibility to tend a pot of pansies? What does it express to her? How does it happen that she is there? "

" I do not see anything in it," said Henri. " It has no action."

" How the devil can it have action before there is a plot? " screamed Jacques. " I tell you, the atmosphere is superb."

"It is a picture, not a story. There is no material in it," complained Henri. "You have everything to create, except the scene. The scene is good, but——"

We were still discussing the question, sipping vermouth at a café, when someone exclaimed: "Ah, you! How goes it?" And, looking up, I saw that the cordial hand upon the dramatist's shoulder pertained to no less eminent a person than Martime himself.

"Numa!" Henri was delighted; the more so when Martime consented to sit down at our table and sip an apéritif, too.

"Permettez. Two of my oldest friends—monsieur Camus, of *L'Elan*; monsieur Rouelle, romancier."

The actor-manager did not allow us to imagine we met upon terms of equality, but his greetings were gracious. To be candid, I had been somewhat impressed to hear our chum call him by his Christian name. I knew, of course, that Henri was agog to learn whether a decision had been reached about his play, and I mentally applauded his air of absorption while Martime expatiated upon his performance in the present piece. After some minutes I glanced at Jacques, with a view to our leaving the pair together, but before we could move, Henri, desirous no doubt of cloaking his eagerness, said lightly:

"As you arrived, we were in the midst of a literary controversy. Monsieur Rouelle detects promise of a great story where I see none. The point is not uninteresting." Whereupon he launched into a description of the street, and did justice to the pansies, though Jacques did not look as if he thought so.

" C'est très bien, ça," said Martime, with weighty nods. " It is very fine, that. Let me tell you that you have there a poem." In no more authoritative a tone could the Academy have spoken.

" Ah ! " cried Jacques. " You feel it, monsieur ? There, in that vile spot, the fairness and fragrance of those pansies——"

" Not ' fragrance,' " said Henri ; " pansies have no smell."

" ——struck a note sensationally virginal," continued Jacques, with defiance.

" Oui, oui," concurred Martime. I suppose it was no trouble to him to do these things, but the ideality he threw into his eyes was worth money to see. We all regarded him intently, and I think he liked the situation. Even more ideality flooded his gaze, and he propped a temple with two fingers. " I am not of your opinion, mon cher," he told Henri profoundly. " I find it admirable."

" The three questions that besiege one, monsieur," burst forth Jacques—and I shuddered—" are, who, biding amid decay, has the imperishable sensibility to tend a pot of pansies ? Of what does it speak to her ? How comes it that she is there ? "

And now it was that the famous man was tempted to a fall.

" Tout à fait admirable," he repeated. " But " —he displayed a cautionary palm—" above all,

Q

no melodrama! The keynote is simplicity. Simplicity and tenderness. For example, in the squalid room sits a young girl, refined though poor— a sempstress. She dreams always of the sylvan vales that she has left, and the lover who is seeking for her. And—it would be very charming—one day the lover passes the window while she waters the pansies."

" Oh, my dear Numa, bosh ! " exclaimed Henri genially.

No sooner had he said it than he recognised his error, I am sure. Martime's eyes flashed poniards, and his face turned turnip colour with offence. Perceiving his indignation, Jacques began to stammer hasty insincerities, and Henri also did his utmost to palliate the affront, but I could not persuade myself that their efforts were successful. For a minute or two Martime remained stiff and monosyllabic, and then, with a few formal words, got up and went.

" I fear he was annoyed," murmured Jacques.

" You ' fear ' ! " said Henri irascibly. I was dismayed to hear resentment in his tone.

Though Martime had gone the constraint continued ; and it was not long before we rose.

As Henri and I walked on, after Jacques had parted from us, I said : " Very stupid of Martime. You spoke in quite a friendly way."

" And still more stupid of Jacques to talk about the story to him," he flung back, at white heat. " What possible interest could Jacques' difficulties have for Martime ? Childish ! "

" But—pardon me, it was you who first mentioned the matter," I said.

" Ah, don't split straws," he growled. Clearly, the incident disturbed him more than a little.

It was probably a week or ten days afterwards that Jacques came to me in great perturbation and volleyed, " What do you think? Henri has got his knife into me! It appears that Martime has returned the play, and Henri says it is my fault."

" Oh, nonsense!" I said. " How can he say that? Returned the play? I am dreadfully sorry."

" I too. But what have *I* got to do with it? Did you ever hear anything more preposterous? To begin with, it is not likely that Martime would refuse the piece solely on account of what was said that day; and, even if he did so, it was not I who said it. It wasn't till yesterday I knew there was anything wrong. Blanche met Elise. Elise's manner was rather strange, and Blanche wondered. But she had no idea there was any ill-feeling. Naturally! She inquired if Henri had heard from Martime yet. Then it came out."

" That Henri held you responsible? "

" Blanche was condoling. She said, ' What a cruel disappointment for you both, dear!' And Elise said coldly, ' Yes, indeed; it is very unfortunate that Jacques discussed his affairs in front of Martime.' Blanche, poor girl, was thunderstruck. Of course, she explained to Elise exactly what had happened. But Elise replied with something very vague, and when I telephoned to Henri he was not himself with me at all—he was very brusque. He said, ' I have no wish to talk about the matter.' There is not the least doubt that he is angry."

" I will have a chat with him," said I.

I went the following day. But he had gone to have a Turkish bath, and Elise, who received me, begged me not to mention the play when I saw him. " His finest work, that took him a year to do, practically wasted ! " she said, in a stunned fashion. " It is frightful. He is stricken. It would be kinder of you not to say anything about it to him yet awhile. I'll tell him that you came."

" But ' practically wasted ' ? " I demurred. " He will be able to place it with some other management, will he not ? "

" He may. But it is not the kind of play for every management. And, anyhow, we shall not get Martime in the part. It will never now be the immense success that it *would* have been. What an idiot to reject a great part because his vanity was wounded ! "

" You are certain that is the explanation ? "

" There is no question about it. The script was returned in the most formal way—a line to say it was ' unsuitable.' Henri was prostrate. Prostrate. My poor Henri ! You may realise what a blow it was. I am feeling very anxious about him. I have persuaded him to go away for a few months— I am taking him to Biarritz. What a calamity his meeting Jacques that afternoon ! "

" Ah, but listen," I urged. " Jacques is terribly

cut up that Henri is bitter against him. And, between ourselves, it is a shade unjust. It was not Jacques who affronted Martime, nor even Jacques who first referred to the subject. It was Henri himself."

" Henri made a passing allusion," she protested; " Jacques made an eternal discussion of it. He would never let it drop. Henri is never unjust, he is fairness itself; I have never known anyone who was as fair as Henri always is. Also, he is not ' bitter ' against Jacques—we are not so small-minded that we forget old friendships because of an indiscretion. When we come back I shall, of course, go and see Jacques and Blanche as usual. I have nothing against Blanche—it was not *her* fault that Jacques was so tactless."

Oh, well. Useless to try to convince people of what they don't want to believe ! I told Jacques that she and Henri were going away, and predicted that he would find the unpleasantness over when they returned. And, as a matter of fact, I did not attach deep importance to it until a certain morning. The sight of a prospectus led me to inquire of Jacques if the shares he had been counting on were allotted to him. He answered passionately, " No."

At that I was startled. I asked if he had made an application for them.

" I did not see anything about it soon enough ! " he raged. " Henri had told me to leave it all to him. And not a word have I had from him. Even if I *had* applied, I should not have got them.

What malice ! Blanche is broken-hearted. I will
never forgive him for her grief. It is not as if I
had been seeking a gift at his hands—he could have
made money for us without its costing him more
than a postage stamp. An opportunity to do such
a service for a friend comes to a man once in a
lifetime. No; his spite against me for nothing is
so intense that deliberately he turns his back on the
chance ! It is disgusting. We could not believe,
we could not think it possible he had been such a
swine, after all his promises. So I got his address
from the bonne and telegraphed to him. You
should see his answer—the letter of a stranger :
' On consideration, he had not cared to take the
responsibility of recommending an investment to
me.' Liar ! Blanche cried the whole night through.
I will never speak another word to him as long as I
live. And I do not want to see Elise either.
Blanche's own cousin, to show such animosity !
What a despicable pair ! "

"Words will not express my regret," I said.
"And I am amazed at Henri's attitude. But
you cannot be sure that Elise knows anything
about it."

"Why should she not know ? " he scoffed.

"I do not suppose that Henri can feel very proud
of himself—he may not have confided in her.
Besides, Elise said she meant to go on seeing you,
the same as ever. That being so, she would hardly
encourage him to break his word to you in the
meanwhile. I think you are being unfair to Elise."

"Henri has been more unfair to my poor

Blanche," he bellowed. " I do not hear so much of your sympathy for *her*."

It was an infamous reply to make, but he was in the mood to quarrel with anyone that was handy, and I had the magnanimity to let it pass. I was sympathising sincerely with Blanche, and I sympathised even more when I saw her. She spoke with less vehemence than Jacques, but it was evident he had not exaggerated her dejection. " It seems incredible," she said. " It shows that you never really know anyone; nothing could have persuaded me that Henri had it in him to behave so badly. If you had heard him talking to us about the shares—what a benefit they would be to us ! And now, to avenge himself for an imaginary wrong——" She gave a gulp. " You don't think Elise knows ? Ah, yes; he and she are one in everything, I assure you ! What it would have meant to us, to get dividends ! However small the sums might have been, what a godsend to poor Jacques, driving his pen all day ! He is working harder than ever to make up for lost time—he has had to put the thought of the pot of pansies aside for the present—and I could cry as I watch him. By the way, you were going to try to find a plot for that. Did you ? "

" Nothing occurred to me," I said.

I could say nothing to cheer her, either then, or later, though I often looked in at the flat and did my best. And, to inflame the indignation, the shares rose. They rose, and went on rising. And Jacques, who had hitherto never so much as glanced at closing prices, developed a morbid interest in following their advance. I shall not forget the day, about three months after the issue, when I learnt that they were quoted at forty francs, and that, if Henri had kept his word, my host and hostess would have doubled their capital. I shall not forget it for two reasons. 1. The lamentations they gave way to were exceedingly trying to me. 2. On that very afternoon Elise walked in.

I had not known that she was back, else I should have prepared her for the situation. Blanche, ignoring the proffered embrace, tendered the tips of her fingers, and Jacques bowed, as to a woman he had never seen before. Elise turned very pale. Her scared eyes sought mine, and I tried by the warmth of my greeting to mitigate the moment for her.

" What is the matter? " she faltered of us all.

" It is only surprise at your visit," said Blanche sarcastically.

Impossible to avert it. The storm broke.

Just as I surmised, Elise had been unaware of Henri's misdeed. But though her consternation was only too apparent, Jacques and Blanche were in no mood to let it influence them. The tirade against Henri to which Jacques condemned her was bad to bear. She quivered under it. She could do nothing but stammer painfully, " I forbid you to insult my husband; I forbid you to insult my husband ! " Blanche knew how to stab, too, in her pathetic voice.

" Ah, it is useless to talk, Elise," she sobbed.

" As a rich woman, you do not understand what three thousand francs would have done for us ! Three thousand francs ! We have been scraping for eight years to put by as much as that, and if Henri had been fair to us we should have doubled our means already. Three thousand francs ! To Jacques, who in all his life has never had a sou that wasn't wrung out of his poor tired head ! It is the wickedness towards *him* that I resent—towards him, and our child. And what is the cause? That Henri is unmanly enough to hate another for his own mistake. Ah, it is too petty and contemptible of him for words ! "

" But remember it is not Elise's fault," I begged. I saw that she could endure no more. " Say these things to Henri, both of you, if you must—not to her ! "

" Blanche is in no need of your corrections," shouted Jacques hysterically. " Attend to your own affairs. My wife talks to her cousin as she thinks fit. It is always Elise you champion. If you feel so deeply for our enemies, I wonder that you come here."

I could scarcely credit my ears. But I said very quietly, with dignity, " Indeed? I shall not put you to the trouble of wondering twice."

And, as Blanche remained silent—for which she was very culpable, for I looked towards her as I moved—I offered my arm to Elise, who was so much deranged that she could hardly get down the interminable staircase, and took her home in a cab.

As will be readily understood, I had no ambition

to assist at her next conversation with Henri, and I did not intend to enter the house. Unluckily, when the cab stopped, he was on the veranda, and he came to the gate.

" *Comment ?* What is it ? " he demanded, seeing her agitation.

" She is rather upset," I said. " I won't come in."

" Yes, yes, come in ! Tell him what has happened," gasped Elise peremptorily. Whereby she, in her turn, committed a grave fault, for she made me witness matrimonial dissension of which I need otherwise have had no knowledge.

" She has been to see Jacques and Blanche," I said, following them into the salon.

" Ah ? " said Henri, with reserve.

" Yes, I have been to see Jacques and Blanche," she panted, " and a nice time I have had there ! "

He decided on hauteur. " I am quite at a loss. If one of you will explain ? "

As she looked at me, I said : " They told her you had not done as they expected about the shares. I rather gathered that there was some tendency towards feeling hurt."

" Hurt ? On reflection, I saw that I had not the right to advise Jacques to speculate. What of it ? "

" They do not view it as a speculation," I said.

" They ! Much they know of business ! "

" Did you take shares yourself ? " queried Elise.

" The cases are not parallel," he contended, his voice rising excitedly. " Jacques is a poor man ; I did not feel justified in letting him risk money."

" Oh, Henri," she wailed, " you know very well

that was not the reason. It was not loyal of you; it was very, very wrong. Already it would have been a little fortune for them. No wonder they are aggrieved. I cannot be surprised—much as I have suffered this afternoon, I cannot be surprised at what I have had to hear."

"What you have had to hear? You have heard that I did not choose to assume the responsibility of conducting another man's affairs. And then? Ah, je m'en fiche! I am fed up with Jacques."

"I have had to hear you broke a promise because you were mean-spirited enough to blame him for your own *gaffe* to Martime," she cried. "Of my husband I have had to hear that! No, I cannot be surprised at what they said. They said it was petty and contemptible of you—*and so it was!*"

For an instant it was as if she had hurled a thunderbolt. Henri stood inarticulate, his eyes bulging from his head. Then, bringing his fist on to the table with a blow that made every ornament in the room jump, he roared :

"You dare to say it? To me, your husband, you dare to say such a thing? You shall ask pardon at once, in the presence of the friend who has heard the insult!" And, as it was obvious she would do nothing of the kind, he went on, without loss of time, "No! I forbid you to apologise— it is vain. There are insults that apologies cannot abate. A husband who is 'contemptible' to his wife is best apart from her—I can find comprehension elsewhere."

I was having a pleasant day—what with one ménage and the other, I was having a pleasant day. There ensued a quarrel the more harrowing from the fact that the recriminations poured from a pair whom I knew to be, at heart, lovers. And as often as I endeavoured to steal out, either Henri or Elise would pounce upon me to confirm some point that did not matter. When I got away at last my need of stimulant was insupportable.

I had, naturally, expected to receive a penitent missive from Jacques that night, and when there was a knocking at my door I did not doubt that he had come to beg forgiveness in person. But it was Henri who flung in, and dropped into a chair.

" Enfin, I go back no more," he groaned.

He took my breath away.

" You are mad," I stuttered. " What? You part from a wife you adore, and who adores you, because of a hasty word? Are you a boy, to behave so wildly? *C'est inouï !* "

" There are words, and words ! " His face twitched and crumpled. " It is because I am not a boy that I see clearly we could never again be happy together. The madness would be to try ! To sit, every day, opposite a woman who is thinking me contemptible? Merci ! I could not endure it. Every meal, every moment would become a hell."

" Ah, if she were thinking it, really ! But she spoke impetuously—she had had much to try her. She had only just left Jacques and——"

" Ah, mon Dieu, mon Dieu, what I owe to that man ! " he vociferated. " What everlasting afflictions, his telling me of his accursed pansies ! First, it annihilated my prospects, and now it rends me from my wife and children. I shall stipulate that they live with me for half the year; but what of the other half, while they are being taught that the father who loves them so dearly is a contemptible man, disgusting to their mother ? " He rocked to and fro. " Also, how am I to make a home for them when they come ? I leave the villa to Elise; I cannot afford two establishments— above all, now that I have lost the production by Martime, and may never see a sou from work that has occupied me for a year. Malediction on that pot of pansies ! "

" Now listen ! " He had been to the last degree unreasonable, but he was suffering, and I have a good heart. " I guarantee that this separation will not last a week. I shall have a talk with Elise."

" With Elise ? It is I who make the separation," he objected, with a piteous attempt at dignity. " And further, I have no hostility against you, but it is partly through your own talks with Elise that she is lost to me. Ah, yes ! " I had stared at him, stupefied. " I understand that you said to her, at the time, that I was guilty of ' injustice ' towards Jacques. I do not say you traduced me with any vicious motive, but, unquestionably, your irresponsible chatter paved the way to the catastrophe that wrecks my life."

My turpitude notwithstanding, he wept in my room till 3 a.m., keeping me up. And he, and Elise, too, proved very distressing to me during the days that followed. She was equally headstrong. I was surprised at her.

" You mean well, but pray say no more; it is inevitable," she answered me tremulously. " As for that stupid affair of Jacques and Blanche, I daresay I may have misjudged Henri. They don't understand. As a business man, no doubt he did what was really best in their own interests." I perceived that her commiseration for them had much decreased since it involved her in domestic strife. " But his conduct towards *me*— ! I have done with him. I am not a fool, to imagine an honourable man would desert his wife for a reason like that. A performance. He did not even forget his razor strop. Let him go to her ! He was not an angel—no writing man is—but I thought he loved me, and I never complained. Because I admired him, because he was the one man in the world to me. Behind the curtain it hung, not even in sight, and he did not forget it when he packed ! Brute ! You heard him say he could ' find comprehension elsewhere.' She will not keep his linen in such order as *I* have done, that I'll swear. To pretend it was just because I believed what Jacques and Blanche had said ! I believe nothing that they say. I detest them. Oh, they have made a pretty mess of my life, those two ! "

She was illogical, but I was much displeased with Jacques and Blanche myself. The previous day

I had seen them in the street. It is true that they cast ingratiating glances, but in the circumstances they should have done a good deal more. And I, very properly, looked away.

Yes, for fully three weeks the estrangement of Henri and Elise made demands on my time. And since each of them viewed the other as the aggressor, their criticisms of each other were not unduly diffident. Nevertheless I continued to do all in my power for them. I implored Henri to return, and I besought Elise to write to him, though it was no recreation to me to keep pressing counsel upon people who told me they did not want to hear it. When there were two consecutive days without Henri despairing in my chair, the lull was welcome.

I cannot depict my joyful surprise, the next evening, on seeing them issue radiantly from the Restaurant Noël Peters, arm in arm. I had had no news of the reconciliation. I rushed to them and clasped their hands.

" Hurrah ! " I exclaimed. " Thank goodness ! How delighted I am the trouble is over ! "

Their greeting appeared to me a shade constrained.

" Oh, that didn't amount to much," Henri mumbled, brushing my reference aside.

" No one supposed it did," laughed Elise lightly. And as I found myself at a loss what to say next, there was a pause.

" We are going to a theatre," said Henri; " we are rather late." After a glance at his wife, he

added, in flat tones, " You will dine with us one
night, hein? "

" Ah, yes," said Elise perfunctorily. " Of
course."

When I went, we did not allude to what had
happened. Nor was the conversation on general
topics as animated as when I had dined there
hitherto. For the first time at their table I was
depressed.

And it was the last invitation from them I
received. Probably I was embarrassing to them,
by reason of their having railed against each other
to me while they thought they would never make
it up. Also, though Henri could forgive his admiring wife for once calling him petty and contemptible,
one may be sure it was bitter to him to remember I
had been present when she humiliated him. That
both he and Elise resented my sharing the secret
of their separation was as clear as daylight. For
some months afterwards, if I chanced to meet
them, they would stop and exchange a few words
with me, but by and by they contented themselves
with smiling; and, finally, they preferred to pass
without perceiving that I was there. When that
play of Henri's was produced, two or three years
later, he had become so alien to me that I should
never have dreamed of going to see it, if I had not
got in for nothing. The leading man was not
capable of the part, and the run was short—by
which Henri's enmity against Jacques was doubtless
intensified.

The two couples that used to be so intimate

remain at daggers drawn. And both couples are
strangers to *me*. I do not think there is anything
to add, excepting that the story of the pot of
pansies has not been accomplished to this day.
The tragic history that I have related is the story
of the story that was never found.

R

XIV

FLOROMOND AND FRISONNETTE

FLOROMOND and Frisonnette, who were giddy with a sense of wealth when they acquired three rooms, and had flowers growing on their own balcony, and sat upon chairs that they had actually bought and paid for, held a reception one fine day. The occasion was a christening. Floromond and Frisonnette were, of course, monsieur and madame Jolicœur, and they dwelt in the part of Paris that was nearest to Arcadia. Among those present were monsieur Tricotrin, the unadmired poet, monsieur Pitou, the composer of no repute, monsieur Lajeunie, whose stirring romances so rarely reached a printing office, and monsieur Sanquereau, the equally distinguished sculptor.

Though the company were poor in pocket, they were rich in benevolence, and since the dearth of coppers forbade silver mugs, they modelled their gifts upon the example of the good fairies. Advancing graciously to the cradle, the bard bestowed upon the female infant the genius of poesy : " Epics, and odes," he declared, " shall fall from her lips like the gentle dew from Heaven." " And, symphonies," said the musician, " she shall drop as nimbly as the newly rich drop

needy friends." That she might be equipped more
fully yet for the stress of modern life, the novelist
endowed her with the power of surpassing narra-
tive, while the sculptor, in his turn, contributed
to her quiver the pre-eminence of Praxiteles.

Then Frisonnette hung over her baby, saying,
" And one boon, besides : let her marry her sweetheart and always remember that a husband's love
is better than an ermine cloak ! "—an allusion
which moved Floromond to such tenderness that
he forthwith took his wife in his arms, regardless
of us all; and which reminded your obedient
servant of their story.

When Floromond beheld her first, she was in
a shop window—the most tempting exhibit that
a shop window had displayed to him, in all his
five-and-twenty years. If he had stayed in the
quarter where he belonged, it would not have
happened. It was early on a spring morning,
and she was posing a hat, for the enticement of
ladies who would tread the rue La Fayette later
in the day. Floromond, sunning himself like a
lord, though he was nothing better than a painter,
went on to the Garden of the Tuileries, noting how
nicely the birds sang, and thinking foolish thoughts.
" Had I a thousand-franc note in my pocket,
instead of an importunate note from a washer-
woman," ran his reverie, " I would go back and
buy that hat; and when she asked me where it
was to be sent, I would say, ' I do not know your
name and address, mademoiselle.' Then, having

departed, without another word, leaving her speechless with amazement and delight, I should never
see her any more—until, not too long afterwards,
we found ourselves, by accident, in the same
omnibus. Ciel! how blue her eyes were."

And, though he did not omit to reprove himself,
in the most conscientious manner, and the weather
changed for the worse, his admiration drew him
to the rue La Fayette, at the same hour, every
day.

Frisonnette's demeanour, behind the plate glass,
was propriety itself. But she could not be unconscious that the young man's pace always slackened
in the downpour, as he approached madame
Auréole's—she could not be insensible of the homage
of his gaze. That Tuesday morning, when, drip-
ping, he bowed, his salutation was so respectful
that she felt she would be inhuman to ignore it.

So the time came when they trod the rue La
Fayette together, making confessions to each other,
after the shop shut.

" I used to wonder at first whether you noticed
me as I went by," he told her wistfully.

" I noticed you from the beginning," she owned,
" you have such a funny walk. The day that you
were late——"

" My watch was in pawn. Sapristi, how I raced!
It makes me perspire to think of it."

" I took five minutes longer than usual to dress
the window, waiting for you."

" If I had guessed! And you didn't divine
that I came on purpose? "

She shook her head. " I used to think you must be employed somewhere about."

" What ! you took me for a clerk ? " asked the artist, horrified.

" Only at the start. I soon saw you couldn't be that—your clothes were too shabby, and your hair was so long."

" I could have wished you to correct the impression by reason of my air of intellect. However, to talk sensibly, could the prettiest girl in France ever care for a man who had shabby clothes, and a funny walk ? "

" Well, when she was beside him, she would not remark them much," said Frisonnette shyly. " But I do not think you should ask me conundrums until you have talked politics with my aunt; I feel sure she would consider it premature."

" Mademoiselle," said Floromond, " I am rejoiced to hear that your aunt has such excellent judgment. Few things would give me greater pleasure than to agree with her politics as soon as you can procure me the invitation."

And one day Floromond and Frisonnette descended the steps of a certain mairie arm in arm— Frisonnette in a white frock and a flutter—and the elderly gentleman in the salle des mariages, to whom brides were more commonplace than blackberries, looked after this bride with something like sentiment behind his pince-nez. A policeman at the gate was distinctly heard to murmur, " What eyes ! " And so rapidly had the rumour of her fairness flown, that there were nearly as many spectators on the sidewalk as if it had been a marriage of money, with vehicles from the livery stables.

The bride's aunt wore her moire antique, with coral bracelets, and at breakfast in the restaurant she wept. But, as was announced on the menu, Wedding couples and their parties were offered free admission to the Zoological Gardens; pianos were at the disposal of the ladies; and an admirable photographer executed GRATUITOUSLY portraits of the couples, or a group of their guests. At the promise of being photographed in the moire antique, a thing that had not occurred to her for thirty years, the old lady recovered her spirits; and if Tricotrin, in proposing the health of the happy pair, had not digressed into tearful reminiscences of a blighted love-story of his own, there would have been no further pathetic incident.

Floromond and Frisonnette, like foreigners more fashionable, " spent their honeymoon in Paris," for, of course, Frisonnette had to keep on selling Auréole's hats. Home was reached by a narrow staircase, which threatened never to leave off, and after business hours the sweethearts—as ridiculously enchanted with each other as if they had never been married—would exchange confidences and kisses at a little window that was like the upper half of a Punch and Judy show, popped among the chimney-pots of the slanting tiles as an afterthought.

" It is good to have so exalted a position," said Frisonnette; " there is no one nearer than the angels to overlook us. But I pray you not to mention it to the concierge, or our rent will soon be as high as our lodging. The faint object that you may discern below, my Floromond, is Paris, and the specks passing by are people."

" They must not pass us by too long, however, Beloved," said Floromond; " I am a married man and awake to my responsibilities. It would not suit me, by any manner of means, to share you with millinery all your dear little life. More than ever I have resolved to be eminent, and when the plate glass can never separate us again, you shall have dessert twice a day, and a bonne to wash the dishes."

" My child," murmured Frisonnette, " come and perch on my lap, while I talk wisdom to you, for you are very young, and you have been such a little while in Paradise that you have not learnt the ways of its habitants. It chagrins you that you cannot give me dessert, and domestics, and a cinéma every Saturday night. But because I worship you, my little sugar husband, because every moment that I pass away from you, among the millinery, seems to me as long as the rue de Vaugirard, I do not think of such things when we are together. To be in your arms is enough. Life looks to me divine— and if I find anything at all lacking in our heaven, it is merely a second cupboard. Now, since you are too heavy for me, you may jump down, and we will reverse the situation."

" I have strange tidings to reveal to you," said Floromond, squeezing the breath out of her— " I adore you, Frisonnette ! "

They remained so blissful that many people were of the opinion that Providence was neglecting its plain duty.   Here was a thriftless painter daring to marry a girl without a franc, and finding the course of wedlock run as smooth as if he had been a prosperous grocer with branches in the suburbs ! The example set to the Youth of the quarter was shocking.   And a year passed, and two years passed, and still the angels might see Floromond and Frisonnette kissing at the attic window.

Then one afternoon it happened that a French beauty, hastening along the rue La Fayette with tiny, toppling steps, as if her bust were too heavy for her feet, found herself arrested by a toque on view at Auréole's—and entering with condescension, was still more charmed by the assistant who attended to her.   The chance customer was no one less important than the wife of Finot— Finot the dressmaker, Finot the Famous—and at dinner that night, when they had reached the cheese, she said to the great man :

" My little cabbage, at a milliner's of no distinction I have come across a blonde who could wipe the floor with every mannequin we boast.   She is as chic as a model, and as bright as a sequin ; she is just the height to do justice to a *manteau ;* her neck would go beautifully with an evening gown ; and she has hips that were created for next season's skirt."

" Let her call ! " said the great man, adding a few drops of kirsch to his *petit suisse.*

" She would be good business, I assure you,"

declared the lady; " she talked me into taking a toque more than twice the price of the one I went in for—*me* ! Well, I shall have to find a pretext for speaking to her—I must go back and see if there is another hat that I care to buy."

" It is not necessary," replied her husband; " go back and complain of the one you bought."

So the lady talked to Frisonnette in undertones, and Frisonnette listened to her in bewilderment, not quite certain whether she was twirling to the top of her ladder, or being victimised by a diabolical hoax. And the following forenoon she passed by appointment through imposing portals that often she had eyed with awe. And Finot, having satisfied himself that she had brains as well as grace— for they are very wide of the mark who think of his pampered mannequins as elegant mechanical toys—signified his august approval.

Frisonnette went home and described the splendours of the place to Floromond, who congratulated her, with a misgiving that he tried to stifle. And later on she told him of the dazzling déjeuners that were provided, repasts which she vowed stuck in her throat, because he was not there to share them. And, not least, she sought to picture to him the gowns that she wore and sold. O visions of another world ! There are things for which the vocabulary of the Académie Française would be inadequate. Such clothes looked too celestial to be touched. But she was a woman. Though her head was spinning, as Finot's mirrors reflected her magnificence, though she was admiring herself

Frisonnette who formerly had run to greet him at the top.

"You are a devoted companion," she would remark bitterly, as he entered. "What do you imagine I do with myself, in this hole, all the evening, while you stay carousing outside?"

"I imagine you sit turning up your nose at everything, as you do when I am with you," he would answer, hiding his pain.

Then Frisonnette would cry that he was a bear; and Floromond would retort that her own temper had not improved, which was certainly true. And after she had exclaimed that it was false, and stamped her foot furiously to prove it, she would burst into tears, and wonder why she remained with a man who, not content with forsaking her for cafés, came home and calumniated her nose, and her temper besides.

Meanwhile Finot had been contemplating her performances on the Aubusson carpet with rising respect. His versatile mind was now projecting the winter advertisements, and he determined to entrust to his best blonde one of those duties which, from time to time, rendered the luckiest of his mannequins objects of unspeakable envy to all the rest. Finot's advertisements were conducted on a scale becoming to a firm whose annual profits ran into millions of francs.

"Mon enfant," he said to her, "you have been a very good girl. And though you may think you are rewarded royally already, as indeed you are" —and here followed an irritating dissertation upon

the softness of her job, to which she listened with
impatience—" I am preparing a treat for you of
the first order. How would it please you to travel,
for a couple of months or so, a little later on? "

" To travel, I? " she stammered.

" You and one of the other young ladies. Monte
Carlo, Vienna, Rome? "

" Rome? " ejaculated Frisonnette, who had
never dreamed of reaching any other " Rome "
than the one on the Métropolitain Railway.

" Mademoiselle Piganne would contrast most
effectively with your tints, I think? " He screwed
up his eyes. " Y-e-s, we could hardly evolve a
colour scheme more delicious than you and mademoiselle Piganne! Whatever capitals we may
decide on, you will stay at the hotels of the highest
standing; all matters like that you will do best to
leave to the judgment of the chaperon in attend-
ance on you both, otherwise you might have the
unfortunate experience to find yourself in an hotel
not exclusively patronised by the cream of Society.
Your personal wardrobe, for which you will be
supplied with from twelve to fourteen trunks, will
consist of those creations of my art which best
express my soul, and your affair will be to attract
sensational attention to them, while preserving
an attitude of the severest propriety. That is
imperative, remember! No English or American
mother, with her daughters beside her, must for a
single instant doubt that you are morally deserving
of her closest stare. An open carriage in the park,
where the climate permits—a stage box at the

opera, when the audience is most brilliant, will, of course, suggest themselves to your mind. But, again, the duenna and the man-servant will organise the programme as skilfully as they will look the parts. All that will be required of you is a display, brilliant and untiring; the rest will be done by others. Every woman everywhere will instruct her maid to find out all about you, and your own maid—an employée of the firm in a humble capacity—will have orders to whisper that you are a princess, travelling incognito, and that your dresses come from Me."

Frisonnette could do no more than pant, " I will speak about it at home, monsieur, at once ! " And because she foresaw with resentment that Floromond's approval would be far from warm, she broached the subject to him very diffidently.

At the back of the little head that Finot's finery had turned, she knew well that if her " bear " betook himself too often to cafés, it was mortified love that drove him to them ; so she made haste to tell him : " It might be the best thing for you, to get rid of me for a couple of months—I should return in a much better humour and you would find me quite nice again."

" You think so, Frisonnette ? " said Floromond, with a sad smile.

" What do you mean ? " she asked, paling.

" I mean," he sighed, " that after the ' brilliant display,' it is not our ménage under the tiles that would seem to you idyllic repose. Heaven knows it goes against the grain to beg a sacrifice, but if you accept such luxury, I feel that you would never bear our straits together again. Do not deceive yourself, little one; you would be leaving me, not for two months, but for ever ! "

Deep in her consciousness had lurked this thought too, and she turned from him in guilty silence. " You are fond of me, then," she muttered at last, " in spite of all ? "

" If I am fond of you ! " groaned Floromond. " Ah, Frisonnette, Frisonnette, there is no moment, even when you are coldest, that I would not give my life for you. I curse the poverty that prevents me tearing you from these temptations and making you entirely mine once more. If I were rich ! It is I who would give you boxes at the opera, and carriages in the park; I would wrap you in that ermine cloak, and pour all the jewels of Boucheron's window in your lap."

" I will not go ! " she cried, weeping. " Forgive me, forgive the way I have behaved. I have been wicked, yes ! But I repent, it is ended—I will not go ! "

And that night she was proud and joyful to think she would not go. It was only in the grey morning that her heart sank to remember it.

" I must decline," she said to Finot hesitatingly. " I have a husband. I—I could not take my husband ? "

" Mon enfant, your husband would not grudge you the little holiday without him, one may be sure."

It was like being barred from Eden. " And the

the flower-vendors at the street corners; and the restaurants, where throngs would fête the *Réveillon*, and New Year's Eve, displayed advice to merry-makers to book their tables well ahead.

"My own rejoicings will be held at home!" said Floromond.

And, during the afternoon of New Year's Eve, it was by a stroke of irony that the first comrade who had rapped at the door since Frisonnette's flight came to propose expenditure. "Two places go begging for the supper at the Café des Beaux Esprits," he explained blithely, "and it struck me that you and your wife might join our party? Quite select, mon vieux. They promise to do one very well, and five francs a cover is to include everything but the wine."

"My wife has an engagement that she found it impossible to refuse," said the painter, huddled over the fading fire. "And as for me, I am not hungry."

The other stared. "There is time enough for you to be hungry by midnight."

"That is a fact," assented Floromond; "I may be most inconveniently hungry by midnight. But I am less likely to be scattering five francs. In plain French, my dear Bonvoisin, if you could lend me a few sous, I should feel comparatively prosperous. I am like the two places at the Beaux Esprits—I go begging."

Bonvoisin looked down his nose. "I should have been overjoyed to accommodate you, of course," he mumbled, "but at this season, you know how it is. What with the pestilential tips to the concierge, and the postman, and one thing and another, I am confoundedly hard up myself."

"All my sympathy!" said Floromond. "Amuse yourself well at the banquet." And he sprinkled a little more dust over the dying *boulets* in the grate, to prolong their warmth.

Outside, big snowflakes fell.

"The man who has never known poverty has never known his fellow-man," he mused; "I would have sworn for Bonvoisin. He has inspired me with an apophthegm, however—let us give Bonvoisin his due! And, to take a rosy view of things, turkeys are very indigestible birds, and, since I lack the fuel to cook it, I am spared the fatigue of going out to buy one for my mahogany to-morrow. Really there is much to be thankful for—the only embarrassment is to know where it is to be found. If I knew where enough tobacco for a cigarette was to be found, I would be thankful for that also. How the Mediterranean sparkles, and how hot the sun is, to be sure! We shall get freckles, she and I. Won't you spare me half of your beautiful sunshade, Frisonnette? Upon my word, I could grow light-headed, with a little encouragement; I could imagine that the steps I hear on the staircase now are hers! Fortunately, I have too much self-control to let fancy fool me."

Nevertheless, as he leant listening, his face was blanched.

The steps drew nearer.

"I know, of course, they go to the room on the